Elendil

Andrea Rose Washington

Acknowledgments

To all my family and friends, to all of my readers Thank you from the bottom of my heart!

Your support and kind words over the years have meant the world to me!

Chapter One

"Hey, Dad," I smiled as I walked into the kitchen pulling my long curly auburn hair into a high ponytail.

"Good morning Darling," my dad, Brenden, smiled over the rim of his coffee mug. "Going for a morning run?" he motioned to my outfit.

"Yep. I'm going to sneak one in before I meet with Macy and Brent to finish our Science project before Monday." I grabbed a bottle of water from the fridge and slipped it into the open pouch on the back of my sports bra. I was a Junior at Hill Crest High and this project was worth at least twenty percent of my grade.

I shivered as the cold bottle touched my skin. "Will you be here when I get back?"

He nodded. "I should be I'm planning to finish a few reports and then relax for the day... I have no reason to head up to the hospital today," he said as he set his cup down. My Dad was on rotation at Hill Crest Community Hospital and had been since we moved here a few back.

"Ok," I smiled. "See you when I get back!" I bounced out of the kitchen and out the front door. I loved to run, and I hadn't had a good one in days, my legs were itching to go. I jumped down the two front stairs and started my jog out of the front yard and down the rest of Elm Street.

My legs carried me down the familiar path; I passed the last five houses before taking a left down Longbranch Avenue. I waved as I passed Mr. and Mrs. Copper, the elderly couple who always baked me my favorite chocolate cake on my birthday, which was weird since they started the year I moved here, and they didn't really know me but the cake was always amazing, so I never complained. I waved as I passed them as they did their daily walk around the block.

My legs pumped as I allowed my mind to drift and let my body carry me down the familiar path of my five-mile run. I ran past Ladybug Park, already full of families enjoying the beautiful Saturday morning. I ran past the community pool that had yet to open and the skate park already full of pre-teens showing off their skills.

I knew a lot of the families here; with my father being an ER Doctor, we regularly had frantic parents coming over to make sure their child was okay after they fell or had a persistent cough. My father never minded though; their visits also helped answer some of the questions they had about our family.

I shook my head as I recalled the shocked faces when my father and I first moved to the community five years ago. My father, a blond hair blue eyed white man – rolled into town with a little girl with a caramel complexion, bright, green eyes, and a head full of auburn hair. They couldn't understand, he was white, and I was black, how?

At first, no one believed him when he told them I was his daughter, well let's just say they didn't want to believe I was his daughter. I was only eleven then, but I still remember the stares I got on moving day and the following days, months, and a select few years after we arrived.

The story the neighbors initially came up with was he adopted me… to them, it was the most logical answer to our varying skin tones. The silence that followed after my father got them to believe I was biologically his daughter was a little unsettling, but since that day, things have improved. I mean I always knew my father and I were different races, I could see it in family photos with my father's side of the family as I never met my mother or anyone on that side. The neighborhood I grew up in always knew and never once made be feel as though I was different. Moving was a huge eye opener for both my father and myself.

I ran down the last hill to the edge of the woods bringing me to the halfway mark of my five miles. I stopped for a few seconds, shook out my muscles, turned around and started my journey back home.

I stopped in front of my house and stretched my arms over my head. I kicked my feet back, quickly stretching out my legs before reaching behind me and grabbing my water bottle out of my sports bra. I took a swig before I ran up the front two steps.

I rolled my neck and reached for the door handle. But before I could grab the handle, the door was yanked open and a tall stranger filled my doorway.

A tall man was standing in the doorway.

A tall man, covered in tattoos, that did not belong at my front door.

I started to take a step back but he was too fast. He reached out a heavily tattooed hand, grabbed my wrist, and yanked me into the house before I could utter a sound.

I looked around my living room and I felt my mouth go dry at sight. There were six men, also covered in tattoos, all wearing black tee shirts and brown cargo pants. Each of them had a gun in their hands. Well, they looked like they were guns, I'd never seen what was in their hands before; they looked like they were picked out on the set of some science fiction show.

"Abriana!" My father's voice rang out.

I sighed in relief as he ran out of the kitchen, he didn't look scared easing my fears only slightly, but he was being followed by a woman. She was tall - taller than me but shorter than my father. She was darker than me, the shade of dark chocolate, but she had the most vibrant green eyes, brighter than my own. Her dark brown hair flowed down her back in tight ringlets. It reminded me of what my hair looked like when I would wash it and just let it air dry; hers was just darker.

"Dad..." I ran to him, hugging him close, instantly feeling safe in his embrace. "What is going on?" I asked him as he held me tightly. I tried to block out the men behind me, but I could still feel their presence blocking our escape. I took a deep breath, trying to remain calm but the feeling of dread still pooled in the pit of my stomach.

My dad squeezed his eyes shut then looked around the room swallowing a few times as his eyes focused on a spot behind me. I knew this tactic; he was searching for the right words to say. I've seen him do this when he's about to deliver some bad news.

"She's gotten so big," the woman whispered staring at me. Her eyes were glistening with, I think, unshed tears.

"They tend to do that as they grow up," my dad hissed at her.

"Dad?" I took a step back, looking at this strange woman then back to him. His body language was tight; he was running his hand through his hair. A clear sign that he was nervous.

"No," I shook my head as the realization slowly dawned on me. She had hair like mine, eyes like mine... it was her.

After all these years - it couldn't be.

"Abriana..." My dad spoke up. "This is your mother, Acadia."

I squeezed my eye shut at his omission refusing to believe him. "You cannot be serious, what's really going on?"

The woman reached her hand out towards me. "Abriana-"

"Don't talk to me." I hissed at her, slapping her hand away from me. Almost instantaneously, a flurry of movement erupted across the room. At once, all of the men stood up and pointed their guns at me.

"You will not raise your hand to the General," the man who opened the door ordered.

"Excuse me?" I scoffed at him. "I'm in my home. You're intruders, in my home. And you're not going to tell me what I can or cannot do," I turned to face her, especially when it comes to someone who claims to be my worthless mother."

"Abriana!" My father's voice bellowed across the room, causing my head to snap to face him instead. "You will watch your mouth."

Confusion spread over me. Did he have the audacity to defend her? Did he yell at me for talking back to *that* woman? That woman who left him when I was three days old and never once reached out, who never gave a damn about him or me?

"Dad, you cannot be serious?!" I asked incredulously. "She left when I was three days old. I do not have to be polite to her."

"Abriana-" the woman tried again, but I did not have it.

"No!" I screamed at her. "Don't talk to me! *You* don't get to talk to me! You don't get to come back with a room full of men with guns and think you can talk to me." I gasped for air as I felt my chest tighten. My dad noticed and caught me as my knees gave out.

"Just breathe," he whispered over and over to me as I tried to collect my breath.

"What's wrong with her?" The woman asked, but I didn't have the air to tell her to shove off.

"She's having a panic attack, a mild one," Dad answered for me. "It happens when she gets stressed."

"She is broken." I heard one of the men whisper, but the woman quickly reprimanded him. At least I thought she did. Her voice was raised, but when she spoke, it was a language I didn't understand.

"Dad," I whispered once I felt my breathing come back to normal. "Tell me the truth, what's going on?"

"Let's talk in the kitchen." He said in a low voice as he stood up and pulled me with him. I kept my head down as we walked away from the room of crazy. I glanced behind me and was relieved that the woman did not follow us. I couldn't bear the thought of her being near me after all this time.

Once we made it to the safety of the kitchen, I ran to the kitchen door, ready to escape. My dad pulled me back.

"Dad what are you doing?" I whispered, trying for the door again. "We need to get out of here!"

He wouldn't budge. "I did not bring you in here to escape." He gently placed a hand on my shoulder. "We need to talk."

I shook my head. "Dad, no this is not happening. We need to leave and get far away from here." I begged.

"You need to calm down and let me explain what's going on." He guided me over to the table, made me sit down, and then took the seat across from me. "I know this is a lot to take in... it's a lot for me as well."

"What's she doing here? Why come back after all this time?"

"I'm not sure of that yet," he rubbed his hand over his face. He looked, well I couldn't figure out how he looked. I've never seen my Dad in this state. He looked so unsure of himself. "She and her team only arrived a few minutes before you got back from your run."

"Well, when are they leaving?" I asked.

"I don't know," he sighed. "But I need you to have an open mind about all of this."

I scoffed. "An open mind? You've got to be kidding me. You want me to have an open mind towards the woman who left us when I three days old? Three days, Dad! How can you even ask me that?"

He sighed. "I know it's not an ideal situation, but we'll never get to the bottom of this if we don't allow her to speak to us."

"Fine," I huffed. Rationally I knew there was no way out of this unless she was heard as she wanted. Once she said her piece, I was kicking her out. "I'll let her explain, but that doesn't mean I'll be nice to the woman while she does it."

"I wouldn't expect you to lay out the red carpet Abriana, but I do expect you to be respectful, I raised you better than that." My dad said.

"I'll try" I nodded reluctantly.

He smiled stood up and reached out a hand to me. "Come on. We can do this, together."

I grimaced but took his hand and stood as well, and we walked back into the living room. The men were still standing around the room, and the woman stood where we left her. There was a tablet floating in front of her and she was typing away on it. I paused looking back at the tablet. It was floating in midair. I looked at my dad, but he didn't seem as shocked by the tablet as I did. Had he seen something like that before? Did she have that when they first met, and better yet, where was she from to have technology that advanced?

He cleared his throat getting her attention. "Why did you come back?"

She stopped typing on the tablet and it folded itself up and flew into her pocket. Again, I looked at my dad expecting some reaction, but there wasn't one. How was he not surprised at all?

"I came back for you Brenden... both of you," Acadia stated firmly. "I was forced to leave after I had you, Abriana. It wasn't something that I planned or wanted to do, but I didn't have a choice at the time. It wasn't safe for me to stay."

"Why not?" My dad asked with his doctor voice. It was calm and collected, but I knew my father. I could hear the strain in his voice. I felt guilt rack my body as it hit me how selfish I was being.

One night a few years ago, after having too much to drink, my aunts finally told me the truth about my father's relationship with my mother. That he fell head over heels in love with my mom and after she disappeared, he was devastated, that he waited weeks for her to come back. And for a while, they did too.

As far as I knew, my father hadn't been in a relationship since she left. Seeing her after all this time must be killing him, and felt my stomach tighten with guilt. I wasn't taking his feelings into account.

"It's not something I can talk about in the open." She glanced around the room. "Not until we are somewhere safe. But for right now, know it was not safe for me to stay and if I had any other option at the time, I would have taken it."

"And so, sixteen years later, you have the option to come back?" My dad asked, and I could hear the doctor voice slipping.

"When I left, I only expected to be away for a few weeks at most. I never planned on being away for years," she explained.

"I don't believe you," I said crossing my arms feeling my blood start to boil at the water down excuse. "You left because you didn't want to be a wife or mother. I don't care why you're here; I don't want you here. I don't want you, and you're not my mother." The words spilled out my of mother before I could stop them. I always had a problem with controlling what I said when I got angry.

"Acadia," Dad said softly and I could hear the years of hurt laced in that one word. "I don't know what you expected, coming here after all this time. You left me- us with no explanation and dropping back in like this," He gestured to the room. "Was a big mistake. I think you need to leave and give us time to think this over." He wrapped his arm around my shoulder and pulled me close.

The woman swallowed, hesitating with her next words. "I understand, and you both have every right to feel that way. You will never know how sorry I am for all the pain I caused, but I am afraid you both misunderstand; I am not here for just a visit. I came here for both of you. To take you back with me. I am not able to leave you behind."

"Are you out of your mind?" I fought back the urge to laugh or cry I couldn't tell right now. "Do you think that is going to work?" I shook my head and walked to the door ignoring the man there. "My dad asked you to leave." I reached for the door but froze when a metal cylinder shot through the window landing in the middle of the room.

Before I had time to question what it was, it exploded, rocking the room and sending me flying back, knocking me into the wall behind me. I fell to the ground, my head exploding in pain as it slammed hard on the hardwood floor.

I felt the heat of the flames eat at my body as I blacked out.

Chapter Two

My head thumped as voices filtered in. I couldn't make out the words; everything sounded muffled. I tried to figure out where I was. I could tell I wasn't on a bed; it almost felt like I was floating but that couldn't be. 'Am I dead?' I wondered. I could be... I tried to open my eyes, but my body wouldn't respond.

Nothing would respond.

My body just floated.

How did one know if they were dead? How does dead feel? But, I couldn't be dead. I'm thinking- that meant I was alive, for now, and that was good enough for me. I tried to remember what happened but I couldn't, it was too hard to think.

I felt sleep call me again, and I allowed it to take me.

When I came to later, I was lying flat on a bed, no longer floating like before. I tried to wiggled my fingers as a test run, they moved only slightly, but that was enough for me. I wasn't dead. I tried to wiggle my toes but no luck, I could feel them I just couldn't move them. 'Ok think Abriana,' I scolded myself. 'What was the last thing that happened?' The last thing I remembered was *that woman* saying she came back for my father and me. I walked to the door to tell her to leave, and then… a fire?

The explosion.

Maybe I *was* dead? I remembered the heat of the blast on my face, the smell of my flesh burning, I remember the initial pain of the flames. I should be gone.

I had to be dead. Right? It was the only answer I could come up with.

I tried to think more on it but I couldn't.

I felt the pull of sleep call me again, and I was out.

When I finally came to again, I heard voices. They weren't muffled like the first time I woke up. This time I could make out my dad's voice, and it sounded like he was arguing with someone, but I didn't recognize who he was talking to. I had to be in the hospital. He must have taken me to the hospital after the explosion. But why would he be arguing with another doctor?

I tried to wiggle my fingers again and smiled as they moved with more ease than before. I decided to push my luck and tried to sit up. I pushed up on my hands, but my body screamed in protest. I let out a small groaned as I relaxed my muscles.

"Abriana!" My dad yelled. I felt the bed dip as he sat down next to me, I could smell his scent.

"Dad?" I struggled to open my eyes, wincing at the bright light.

"Here let me help you." He said helping me sit up slightly. I gritted my teeth at the new position but didn't stop him.

Once I was up slightly, I looked around the room, trying to understand where I was. I could tell I was in a hospital room but never one I'd never seen before. So that means I wasn't at Hill Crest Community. Made sense, they probably weren't advanced enough to handle the burns I knew

I must have. I ignored that woman standing near the door and focused on the room.

The room was sleek and silver and looked like it was ripped from another science fiction show.

I concluded that where ever I was, it had to be state of the art. I closed my eyes for a quick second focusing on my bed, it was soft, like I was lying on a cloud. I remembered when I was younger, sleeping in empty hospital rooms waiting for my dad to be finished with work – the beds there were nice but never this soft. It felt like memory foam deluxe… if there was such a thing.

I tried to sit up more, but my dad stopped me.

"Don't move to much, you're still healing." His voice switched over to his soothing doctor mode.

"Well, I'm not dead. That's a good start." I laughed relishing the pain a bit.

"No, you are not dead," he said his eyes shining with unshed tears. "But I did almost lose you," he whispered before dropping a kiss to my forehead. I fought back my own tears hearing his throat catch, he looked as though he hadn't slept in days looking over me. It made me realize how close to death I came.

"Everything is fuzzy, but I do remember the explosion, Dad." I looked at him. "I was close enough to die.

I remember the heat of the fire," I paused. "I should be dead though, right?"

"...Abriana" he started but I cut him off.

"No," I ignored the pain and pulled the covers back and looked over my body. No burns were covering me, no cuts or abrasions, nothing that would say I was ever near an explosion. "How am I alive, without a single cut or burn to show for it?"

"Your mother..." he said.

"That woman." I cut him off. I still was not ready to call her my 'mother'.

He nodded and kept going. "She has a more advanced way of healing, and without those ways, you would've died."

"How long was I out for?" I asked.

He bit his lip then answered. "Just under two weeks. I wasn't sure if you were ever going to wake up."

I swallowed my surprise, as the daughter of a doctor I knew after an injury of my significance it was expected to be in a medically induce coma. "Was I in water at any point? I remember waking up and floating."

"You woke up then?" he asked in surprise.

I shrugged. "Not for long. Only a few seconds."

He looked like he was trying to gather his thoughts. "They have healing vats here."

"Healing vats?" I asked making sure I heard him correctly.

He nodded. "I almost didn't believe it myself, but they were able to get you in one, and you started healing. You were on the brink of death, and they brought you back."

I saw a tear run down his face; he quickly wiped it away, I tried not to tear up myself. I needed to stay strong for him, if I could.

"Where are we?" I finally asked.

He seemed to debate what to say to answer me, but after a moment he sighed. I took that as a sign he decided to tell me.

"We're on your mother's ship." He said it in a way that I knew he chose his words very carefully.

"Ship?" I pushed. "Like a boat? How? We don't live near water?"

"No... not like a boat." He answered still choosing his words carefully and it was starting to annoy me.

"If not like a boat then what?" I asked. "Dad, I don't understand. What other kind of ship can you be talking about?"

"Abriana," he grabbed my hand in his and held it for a few seconds. He opened and closed his mouth multiple times but no words formed.

"Where are we?" I asked again.

"Her spaceship."

I blinked waiting for him to say, 'got ya' or something along those lines because he did not say what I thought he did. "Dad..." I shook my head.

"I know, I know." He shook his head. "I promise you; I'm telling you the truth."

"If we're on a spaceship then what... that makes her from outer space, and that makes her an alien..." I trailed off feeling the weight of my words fall on me. "Which would make me one."

"Abriana..."

"No." I shook my head. "I'm dead. I must be dead. This is crazy! You can't- I- know I'm not an alien."

"If by an alien you mean not from your planet then yes, I am, and then by extension, you are as well." That woman finally spoke. "There are many other worlds outside of your solar system."

"Get out." I seethed at her.

"Abriana, you need to hear her out," my dad said.

"I don't have to do anything," I glared at her, "and I don't want to be in the same room as her. I. Don't. Want. To. See. Her." I punctuated each word.

"Well, we need to talk, so I think I will stay," she said walking to the other side of my bed. "We have much to discuss before we land."

"Land?" I asked.

"On my world. Elendil."

"Elendil?" I repeated looking at her like she grew two heads.

"It's in the Isildur system. We are about two hundred light years away from Earth. It's where I'm from, where you're from."

"No, I was born on Earth. I'm American." I glared at her. I caught my father's eye and sighed and tried to swallow my growing anger and curiosity at her words and changed the subject. "How long until we get there?" I forced out.

"In a few days. I am glad you have awoken before then. It would be best if I explain to you who I am before we land."

"I remember one the of the men calling you General, back at the house, so I take it you are a General." I knew I was being a smartass, but I was hoping to end the conversation before it started but she just nodded and kept talking.

"Yes, you are correct. I am a General. I run the royal military on Elendil. I am second on the planet only to the royal family, meaning as you are my daughter, you are second only to the royal family. You both are," she motioned to my father.

"Did you know she was an alien when you met her?" I turned to my dad ignoring her explanation and getting to the pressing question I had, but the woman answered for him.

"I did not tell your father who I was..., what I was when we first met. I did not know if I could trust him at the time and once, I knew I could, I told him." She explained.

"You told me the day before you left," dad hissed under his breath. She seemed to hear him but choose not to answer.

"When we arrive on Elendil we will be greeted by the royal family."

I closed my eyes and took another deep breath as my heart started hammering in my chest. She kept talking but it came in muffled. I could feel the start of another panic attack and I refused to have another one in her presence. I felt my Dad's grip tighten on my hand and I quickly counted back from ten and took slow deep breaths. Once I reached one, I felt my heart beat return to normal and opened my eyes again. I missed her whole explanation and if I was honest, I didn't care.

"Are they going to care that we're from Earth?" I asked the next question that popped in my head.

She waved her hand like my question didn't matter. "Elendil is a world built of many worlds. I'm pretty sure we have a few others from Earth living within our nation as well, not many but some."

"Do all alien's all look like you?" I asked the next question that popped up.

"Most are humanoid, but with a galaxy so big and vast there are millions of worlds and millions of different types of aliens."

I pinched myself a few times feeling the pain shoot up my arm. This was actually happening. I was talking to an alien, on an alien ship, heading towards an alien planet and I was half alien.

"Do they all know English?" I asked.

She nodded. "Most do, there are many that travel to Earth for business or vacation. It is a widely known language most anyone you run into on Elendil will at least understand it. We also have an interplanetary translation implant. We have implanted it right behind your ear."

I reach up and felt the small bump behind my left ear.

Before I knew it, the question I really wanted the answer to roll off my tongue. "Why did you leave, and not the answer you gave back at the house, I want a real answer." I squeezed my Dads' hand. "We deserve a real answer."

I could tell she was expecting the question, but she still looked away almost as if she was ashamed. "It's a long story, one that I was only able to tell your father a few nights ago." I ignored the way she looked at my father; I'd seen that look on many women's faces when it came to him. It was annoying growing up. It was annoying still. Especially coming from *her*.

"When I first came to Earth, I never expected to see my homeworld again. I had been exiled, due to circumstances not of my own making. I started making life on Earth, and then I met your father. I was pregnant and in labor when I received word that my exile had been lifted and I was needed back on Elendil. Elendil was at war, fighting off the southern invaders. When the Acting General, the man who trained me, was killed, they rescinded my exile and called me back to take his place. I could not leave my people to die, so I made the hardest decision of my life – to leave once I gave birth to you. I tried to stay as long as I could, and I truly wanted to bring you both with me. But I knew a war zone was the last place either of you needed to be. It was not safe. So," she paused and took a breath. "I had to leave you behind."

"And it took sixteen years for you to come back?" I snorted.

She sighed. "Abriana, war is not easy nor quick. It took nearly ten years for us to regain control and end the war that our southern half started. The last six years were spent rebuilding a world that was ravaged by fighting for so long. We needed to help our people heal; we needed to prove to the other planets in the system that it was safe for them to send ambassadors once more. Once the royal family earned back the trust of its people, I helped stabilize the planet to the point it is at now. I finally felt it was safe enough to come back for you. But it seems like I was too early, I brought my enemies straight to your door."

I stared at her for a moment, unsure of how to respond, or if I should believe her. If she was telling the truth I could see her justification for her actions, but I didn't want to hear it, I couldn't. I knew I was acting like a child, but I couldn't help it, years of hurt and anger directed towards her finally had their outlet.

"What about our life on Earth?" I turned to my dad blocking her from my view. "The explosion. Grandma and Grandpa must be worried. Did you say goodbye?"

"There wasn't time," my dad dropped his head slightly. "When I can, I will get word to them that we are fine and alive."

"And until then, what?" I asked heat rising in my chest. "Just let them think we're dead? Dad, we can't do that to them, to everyone who cares about us."

"I know Abriana, but right now the safest thing for everyone is for us not to have contact. We couldn't risk staying around and letting them attack us again."

"So just like that our life on Earth is over? All because of her? Do I not get a say in the fact that I might not want to live on another planet?"

My dad ran his hand through his hair then pinched the bridge of his nose, I was stressing him out, but I didn't care. "Abriana. There's no easy way to say this, but it's out of our hands for right now."

"You will never know how sorry I am for bringing you two into this." That woman spoke up; she looked visibly upset. "I never intended for our reunion to play out in this manner. I wanted to ease you into all of this."

I rolled my eyes. "You showed up in our house with a group of armed men. That's not easing."

"I see that point. But that was easy compared to the other option."

"Can I ever go back?" I asked and I knew what the answer was going to be, but I had to hear it for myself. I refused to believe I could never go home.

She paused as though she was debating her answer. "I do not know when. It all depends on the information we receive about the attack. I will only allow you to return once I know it is safe and if at that time what you want is to go back, then yes you will be able to go back...both of you." she trailed off looking at my dad.

"Good." I closed my eyes and turned my back to them not wanting to risk looking at either of them. I felt my world end around me. I could tell she was lying and that she was trying to give me hope but I saw right through it I wouldn't being going back to Hill Crest High, see Macy and Brent again and finish our science project. Though now that I was an alien, I could've been the project. We would've gotten an A for sure. Was I ever going to see anyone in my family ever again? Grandma, Grandpa, Aunt B, or my cousins again?

"Ok then." I heard her stand.

"Can you give us a few minutes?" I heard my dad ask.

"Of course," she replied. I heard the door open, and I waited until I heard it close before I turned back to face my father.

"Abriana, there is a lot you don't understand," he said, and I knew while he was still angry with her, he was trying to find a way to forgive her.

But I didn't want to hear it. "She left Dad. At the end of the day she left for sixteen years. No word, no letters, nothing. If you want to forgive her, that's up to you up, but I don't have to."

"No matter what she's done she's still your mother Abriana."

"I'm tired," I whispered, but he knew I just wanted to be alone.

"Ok honey," he said as he leaned forward and kissed my forehead. "I'll be back later to check on you."

"Ok." I pulled the thin cover over tighter around me.

My mother- that woman, was alive and she was an alien.

Years.

I'd waited years for that woman to come back to us. Years for my family to be made whole, but it never happened. Every year on my birthday until I turned twelve, I wished my mother would come home until I finally gave up.

I couldn't let her in. I would only get hurt if I did.

Chapter Three

"Who is this?" I looked between that woman and my father as they let a tall man into my room. When my dad said he would come back to check on me, I assumed he meant alone but no he couldn't give me that, he had to come back with more people.

The man was taller than my father but only by a hair. He had a buzz cut, and there were black tattoos up and down his arms. I recognized him from the house; he was one of the guards.

That woman answered. "This is Vikram. He will be your guard."

"My what?" I asked again.

"Your guard." She repeated.

"Why?" I asked.

"You will need protection while you are with us. The attack at your home shows that we are not as safe as we thought. Vikram will make sure you are safe no matter where you are." She said.

"Am I not safe on this ship?"

"You are, I can account for everyone here, but it will be good for you to get used to his presence. Once we step foot off this ship, he will be at your side. Always."

"Even when I sleep?" I bit out glancing at my dad, and he narrowed his eyes at me.

"This is serious, cut the jokes Abriana." He said.

"Well what about you," I said. "Will you have a guard, if it's so serious."

That woman stood up a bit straighter. "I will be able to protect him."

I wanted to retort, but one look from my father said I should keep my mouth shut. So, I forced a smile and nodded for now. "Fine." I raised my hand in mock salute.

"Good." She said but her eyes narrowed slightly, and I felt a jolt of happiness at annoying her. "We will leave you to get to know each other. We should be landing in a few days.

Vikram will help you learn the layout of the ship." That woman said.

My dad, noticing the tension, spoke up. "I'll come back and check on you later. Though in the meantime I've asked Vikram to help you strengthen your leg muscles. You basically have new legs."

"Fine," I gave him a mock salute as well, repeating my earlier answer. My dad grimaced at my actions but let it go and kissed my forehead again then he walked to the door and opened it up for that woman. She walked out first, and he followed.

Just like that, he left me behind, with just Vikram.

"Well, I guess it's just you and me," I said once we were alone; Vikram nodded. "What should we do?"

"Your father explained, I am to help you learn to walk again," Vikram said repeating my father's words.

"I don't feel like it." I leaned back in my chair; I knew I was acting like a child but I couldn't help myself.

"I do not think your father was offering a suggestion. I believe he was ordering you to practice while they discuss the upcoming days."

"Shouldn't I be there, too?" I asked.

Vikram cocked his head to the side. "Why?"

"If they're discussing the upcoming days, I should be part of the conversion. It's my life they are talking about."

"Your parents..." he started.

"She is not my parent!" I yelled at him cutting him off.

"It is my understanding that she gave birth to you, that would make her part of your parental unit."

"I'm sorry." I choked on a laugh. "Parental unit?"

"I apologize for the misunderstanding. Where I am from, we call our parents 'parental units' but nevertheless, she gave birth to you."

"Yeah, then she skipped town for sixteen years!" I yelled. "She has not earned the right to be called my parent. She has never once been there for me! She doesn't get a say in anything about my life."

"I am sorry you feel that way, but I believe you are incorrect."

"Well, I don't think I am. She walks back into my life, and I almost die."

"That was not her intention." He reasoned and he was correct, but I couldn't hear it.

"I don't care! I know what my skin smells like on fire because of her. She is not my mother. She is not my parental unit. She is nothing to me."

I could see I struck a chord with him and it felt good to be getting a rise out of him as well. I was just this ball of angry. His jaw clenched, and I could see his eye brighten with anger at my words. "You are young. You see the world through the lens of a young child, but you will soon see; the world is larger and more difficult to understand. I will be outside if you need me." He turned on his heels and swiftly walked out of the room, slamming the door behind him. I stuck out my tongue at the closed door and crossed my arms.

I looked out the window, admiring the stars and bright planets that sparkled through the darkness. 'I don't care what he said. I'm not wrong.' I thought to myself as I looked out my window. I would never admit it out loud, but I was a tiny bit excited to be in space. I mean I was in space, there were millions of people who would kill to be where I was.

But the tiny spark of excitement I had was quickly diminished by the fact that I was half freaking alien, compounded by the fact I was only in space because I was headed to that woman's home planet…, and there was a good chance I would never see Earth again.

I wished it was a bad dream; I sighed looking back out at the endless view. I couldn't see anything I recognized in the stars. I mean, I wasn't the best at astronomy, but I could identify most of the major constellations, and I couldn't see any of those formations in the sky. We really were a long way from Earth from home.

I needed to get out of this room. I reached for the wheelchair to my left, but I couldn't reach it. "Ugh," I sighed. I pushed the covers back and tried to roll my body closer to the edge of the bed.

I miscalculated the force of my roll and sent my body tumbling to the ground with a soft thud.

"Could this day get any worse?" I groaned into the floor.

I pushed myself up on my palms and grabbed at the bed, but my hand slipped, and I hit the ground with another thud.

I fumed and rolled myself on my back. I lifted my head slightly and looked at my legs. I focused on my feet and wiggled my toes, barley. "Move." I hissed trying with all my might to get my feet to obey me. They felt like lead trying to move them. My dad was right, I would have to basically learn to walk again. Much to my annoyance.

I must have laid there for twenty minutes before I decided to swallow my pride. I was able to drag my body to my chair, but I didn't have the upper body strength to pull myself up. I needed help. I blew out a breath, he knew I was going to need his help.

"Vikram!" I yelled, hoping he could hear me through the door. "I need your help."

I paused to listen for any movement but heard none, so I tried again. "Vikram!" I yelled a bit louder and waited again to hear if he heard me.

Silence.

I screamed again as loud as I could. "Vikram!"

Finally, I heard movement, and the door opened. Vikram walked in, his head on a swivel, probably attempting to figure out where I had disappeared to. Finally, he looked down at the floor, at me.

"Why are you on the floor?" he asked, and I could swear there was a hint of a smile on his face, as if he wanted to laugh. I wanted to hit him – he had to know why I was there.

I leaned back on my elbows. "Wanted to see the view from down here." I deadpanned. "Can you just help me up?"

"I believe you told me you do not want my help."

If I could have kicked him, I would have. "I know what I said! But I need help now."

"If I help you off the floor, we will do what your father asked. You will practice your walking."

"Are you serious? You would leave me here on the floor if I don't agree?"

He nodded.

I groaned. "I can barely move my legs, how am I supposed to walk?"

"It is a process that will take time and effort." He said, and I rolled my eyes.

"I know, my dad's a doctor. I've seen him with patients before."

"Then you should understand the work that needs to be done. If you want to walk again, you will need to put in the work."

"Fine," I sighed. "Help me up, and I agree we can work on my walking."

Vikram nodded, walked over, and reached out a hand. I took it and, with a strength and quickness I should have expected, he pulled me to my feet. His free hand grabbed my waist to hold me steady as my knees buckled under me. I held on to his forearms to steady myself on my unfamiliar feet.

"We will take this one step at a time," he said holding my arms. I nodded, took a breath and dragged my leg forward.

Chapter Four

I don't remember learning to walk the first time, and really who does, but it couldn't have hurt as much or been as tiring as it was now. Vikram and I had been working on my steps for the past hour, and I was sore in places I never knew I could be. I could only manage a few minutes before my legs would collapse under me. Yet, no matter how many times I collapsed, I never hit the ground – Vikram caught me each and every time.

"Can we take a break," I begged after my last drop. My legs felt so heavy and tight, and I just wanted to sit down for the rest of my life.

Vikram nodded and lowered me in the wheelchair. "Would you like me to leave?"

"No." I shook my head as my stomach rumbled. "I'm hungry. Can you take me to get some food?"

"Yes, Ma'am." He opened the door to my room and walked behind my chair.

"Don't do that, don't call me 'Ma'am'." I shook my head as he pushed me out of the room stopping to close the door behind us. He didn't lock it and I doubt anyone would have entered anyway. "I'm not old enough to be called Ma'am. Just call me Abriana."

"Noted," he said, pushing me down the hall.

He pushed me in silence down a few halls until we reached an elevator. He pressed the down button, and we waited in silence.

It took a few minutes for the elevator to arrive and I played with my hands while we waited for it to come.

"Can I ask you something," I asked as the elevator dinged, signaling its arrival. Thankfully, it was empty, and he pushed me on.

"Yes?" He pressed the lowest button, and the door closed.

"Do you respect her?"

"I would give my life for her. The General has done much for our people. After her return, she was able to turn the tide of the war." I frowned as I heard the respect and admiration in his voice.

"Did she ever mention my father... me?" I wasn't sure how to phrase the question. She kept telling me how much it hurt her to leave us, how it wasn't part of her plan, how it pained her to be separated from us. I needed to know how much of that was really true from someone other than her.

"We knew she had taken a mate." He answered.

"A mate?" Okay, now I was getting confused. "You mean a husband?"

"No." The elevator stopped, the door opened, and he started pushing me forward. "I mean a mate. Many planets and their occupants have a gene that manifests once we see our mate. It only happens when one meets the other being, they are destined to be with."

"And my father is that for... her?" I asked.

"Yes, she would have felt a great pull to him once she met him. He is the only man she will ever truly love."

"That's sweet, tragic, but sweet," I lied. It was not sweet, it was weird. Is it the same for my father? I mean he is from Earth."

"Because they mated, and you were the result, yes. Once someone finds their mate, they are not able to produce children with anyone else."

He stopped in front of some double doors. He turned us around and entered the room backward then turned me around to face the room.

"Wait, so children are only produced within a mated couple? What about couples that are not mates, how do they have children?"

"They are only able to have children with others before they meet their mate. Once you lay eyes on your other half our genetics do not allow for children out side of that union." He replied as he pushed me to a table. "I am going to get you some food." He said walking towards the line. While he walked away, I looked over the small cafeteria; only three other people were sitting at the table on the far side of the room. I recognized one of the men as the one who yanked me into my house; the other was the man who said I was broken when I had my panic attack.

"What are you thinking about?" Vikram's voice pulled me out of my thoughts as he placed a tray of 'food' in front of me.

"Nothing important." I waved it off; I wasn't going to tell him about my panic attacks so he could think I was broken as well. But if he was in the room when I had it, he would already think I was broken.

Wait.

Why did I care what he thought of me?

"Do you think I'm broken?" I asked picking up my fork and poking the white brick on my plate.

"Pardon? I am not sure I understand." Vikram picked up the drink he carried over and took a sip.

"You see that guy over there?" I nodded my head over to the three men still conversing at the other table. "The middle one, I remember him calling me 'broken' when I had a panic attack at my house."

"His name is Jaja, and no I do not think you are broken. I have studied Earth in school; panic attacks are most common among your people. You were receiving upsetting news. It is only natural that you would have a panic attack as your brain tried to process life changing information."

"Oh." I poked at the white brick again. I was not expecting him to give me that explanation. "What do you mean you studied Earth? Aliens study Earth?"

"It is a common subject in most schools as it seems Earth will be the next planet to join The Union of Planet in a few decades."

"Decades?"

"It takes time to ease a world into the understanding that there is life outside of them. We have found, in order to avoid war and distrust, it is best to pull people in slowly."

"Oh." I poked at the brick again.

"That is called Dino Fish," Vikram said.

"It looks like tofu."

"It is not. It is harvested from the Dino Fish on Elendil. It resembles what you call a salmon but is close to four times the size, and it is completely white. It tastes closer to what you call beef."

"Oh." I picked up my knife and cut into it. I took a tentative bite of the small piece and sighed once the flavor hit my tongue. It *was* good, it tasted close to a rib-eye steak, but it had the texture of fish which was throwing me off. But I was starving, so continued to eat it.

"The green mash is close to your potatoes. I did not bring a vegetable over as I know people from Earth are picky about them."

"Did you learn that in your class?" I laughed at my joke. "But that's fine; I *am* picky about my veggies." I took a small taste of the green mash and was pleasantly surprised it tasted like roasted potatoes.

Vikram smiled into his cup but didn't say anything.

Chapter Five

Vikram pushed me down the halls of the ship back towards my room. I'd spent a total of three days on the ship, and I finally was getting used to walking again, and it was happening at a faster rate than I thought possible. Vikram told me it was due to my alien DNA. Our genetic makeup allowed us to heal faster and gain skills at a higher rate than people from Earth. In just three days I went from managing a few steps an hour to being able to walk a mile before getting tired. But I think that had to do with the healing vats. I was in one after each training session, and I always came out feeling like I just woke up from a nap, refreshed.

I wanted to push myself more today, I did miss running, but we were landing in just under and hour, and I needed to change and make myself presentable before then. Since it was the Royal Family greeting us on our arrival, I was told I couldn't do so dressed in leggings and workout top. Before my training with Vikram, I was told that woman was going to lay out a dress for me to wear on my bed.

I had yet to speak to her alone, not that I wanted to, but I did want to talk to my dad away from prying ears. In the past three days I still hadn't had a chance to speak with him about what Vikram told me about them being mates. I just wanted to know why he kept this from me my whole life. He had millions of chances to tell me who she was.

"Are you ok?" Vikram asked as we got closer to my door.

"Yeah, just thinking about the upcoming hours. I've never met a Royal Family before."

"You need not worry," Vikram said. "They are nice. I grew up with the prince."

"Are you a Royal too?" I asked as I turned in my seat a bit to get a good look at his face.

"No," he laughed, "but my father works for the king. I grew up with the Royal Family."

"Oh," I replied, realizing that I never gave any thought to Vikram's life. I never bothered to ask, how incredibly inept of me. "What does your father do?"

"He is one of the King's advisors and has been for most of my life."

"Did you live in the castle, growing up?"

"No, thankfully, but we did live close."

"Why thankfully?" I asked picking up on his choice of words. I'd noticed that Vikram chose his words very carefully when he spoke.

"Not living in the castle afforded me a normal, well as normal as could be during wartime, childhood. I did not have to be on my guard at all times."

"Oh, I guess that's nice," I said.

"It was, but the Royal Family is very understanding. You will enjoy your time there."

"You just said it was great that you didn't have to live there."

"While I was a child," he said. "You are older. You are more in control of your actions. It should be easier for you to act how is required in the public eye."

"Thanks for the vote of confidence." I deadpanned, noting his choice of the word 'should' as we reached my door. I stood out of the chair and opened my door. My eyes traveled to my bed first.

Laying there was a beautiful blue dress. "I will be outside your door should you need anything." Vikram nodded and closed the door for me. I walked forward and dropped on my bed next to the dress and ran my hand over it. It looked like silk and felt like water against my fingers.

I sighed and walked over to the bathroom. I ran my hand along the wall and closed the door behind me. I showered, washed my face and brushed my teeth. Taking my time which each step. Once I felt I was good I walked out to my room and got dressed. Once the dress was on, I admired myself in the full-length mirror and appreciated the image reflected back at me. The dress did feel like water rushing down my skin. I zipped it up best I could, but my arm couldn't extend far enough to pull it the rest of the way.

"Vikram!" I called with my back to my door and he entered a few seconds later. "Can you zip me up?" I asked not bothering to take my eyes off the dress.

"Yes." Vikram walked over to me and pulled my zipper up the rest of the way. I felt my back straighten and the dress got impossibly tighter on my frame.

"What the-" I looked down at the dress. It was no longer loose. The top of the dress formed a sweetheart neckline. The bodice of the dress clung to my frame leaving my figure to no one's imagination. It hugged my hips and ended right at my knees. "This is not the dress that was on my bed."

"It is," Vikram said as he took a step back. "On Elendil, fabric adjusts to the body of the wearer to give them the best fit possible."

"And this is the best fit for me?" I motioned to my body. "I'm not trying to make that good of an impression!"

"You mother is the king's right hand. It is expected for you to look the part."

I rolled my eyes. "I wish I didn't have to live in the castle." Vikram smiled but didn't say anything. I knew he agreed with me, not that he would admit it out loud.

"Come," he motioned to the door. "Your parents are waiting."

"Wait." I sat down on the bed and grabbed the heels at the foot of my bed. I slid them on and strapped them up. "Now I'm ready." I stood, and my legs shook a little. I had yet to wear heels with these new legs. Vikram held out a hand to steady me. Without a word, he walked with me along the hallway to the elevator to take me to the loading dock where we were to exit the ship.

The doors opened, and I saw my father and that woman standing together, too closely.

I paused watching them. I wanted to observe them before they realized I was there. I wanted to know how my father really felt about her. Thankfully Vikram noticed and pulled me behind a few stacks that could hide us a bit more. I gave him a grateful smile and kept watching. I was too far to hear what they were saying, but I knew my dad's mannerisms. Many women, and I mean a sickening amount of them, hit on him in the past and they got nowhere. I could tell by how he stood what he was thinking.

He usually was rigid - straight back, hands to his side or clasped together, and a straight polite face. A pleasant, neutral demeanor that meant he wasn't interested.

But he wasn't like that with her. He was leaning against the wall, smiling at her. A real smile, he was laughing with his eyes in a way I never saw before. He was so relaxed with her; he held on to her hand with his thumb rubbing along her palm.

If I didn't know any better, I could've sworn that he was flirting with her.

"Vikram," I whispered. "Is she a good person? I mean is she a really good person?"

"She is." He answered.

"I've never seen my dad smile like that before. I always wanted him to find someone," I whispered. "I just don't want him to get hurt…, again."

"I do not believe she intends to hurt either of you. You mother has missed you both in ways that you will never understand."

"I guess I have to be an adult about this, huh?" I was still so torn. I wanted to laugh and scream at the same time.

"It would be wise. Again, I have known your mother for a long time. Her heart only belongs to your father; she will never love another."

"Fine." I said taking a breath. "I guess I can give her a chance,"

I couldn't see it, but I swear I heard him smile. I cleared my throat and walked from behind the stacks.

My dad straightened up and dropped her hand as he saw us coming.

"Hi, Dad." I smiled and gave him a small hug. I turned to her and swallowed.

"Hello…, Mother." I saw her face light up just slightly, and Dad reached out and grabbed her hand.

"Hi, Abriana." Her voice wavered slightly, but she quickly cleared her throat and straightened up and gave me a huge smile. I will take this to my grave, but the look on her face made me want to cry and hug her as well.

Chapter Six

A few minutes later I gazed out the window, down to her home planet. The world was beautiful. The city landscape was littered with domes that Vikram told me were used to grow their food away from pollution. The city was filled with tall silver buildings, and on the outskirts, there were hundreds of mansions. Further out from there, were smaller homes that reminded me of the neighborhoods from back home.

At the edge of the city, where we were heading, were the lush grounds that surrounded the castle where my dad and I were going to live for the foreseeable future.

It was large, about at least four times bigger than Buckingham Place not that I ever saw that particular palace in person.

"Almost there," my dad whispered next to me as the ship started its descent. I shifted from side to side on the balls of my feet smoothing down my dress. My father was wearing a dark blue suit with a white shirt and matching blue tie. My mother was wearing a long dark blue dress that paired my father in color but mine in shape. I had to admit to myself that if I got my genes from her I was going to age well.

The ship jarred slightly as it connected to the dock and my mother stood up a bit straighter. My father mimicked her. We stood a few minutes before the ship's door started to open.

I raised my hand to shield my eyes from the bright light that began to seep in. My mother started walking down the ramp, and my father and I walked alongside her.

"Your Grace," she said as she bowed her head. My father and I followed suit as we reached the Royal Family standing to greet us. "May I introduce my..." She paused as if she was not sure of the next words she was going to say. "My family. My mate, Brenden, and our daughter Abriana."

"It is an honor to meet you, your Grace." My father said bowing slightly again.

The King smiled and nodded. He was on the taller side with dark skin, broad shoulders and dark piercing eyes and full lips. His presence oozed power and I felt slightly intimidated just standing in front of him. "The honor belongs to my family; we are honored to have you here. Allow me to introduce my wife, Queen Zadra," She was about a head shorter than her husband, with soft healthy curves and caramel colored skin with almond shaped hazel eyes. She radiated a sense of calm, but her eyes told another story. "and our son, Nasol." He was a work of art. He was the perfect mix of both of his parent's complexions. He was a hair taller than his father with broad muscles that bulged under his shirt, but he had his mother's almond hazel eyes. There was something about him, but I couldn't put my finger on it. "And I am your humble King, Ezir." He finished with a cheeky smile. Nasol, however, rolled his eyes at his father's introduction. Our eyes met briefly before I saw his eyes sweep over my body and I was suddenly self-conscious over how tight my dress was.

"Thank you for your hospitality, your Grace. Allowing my family to stay here, it is most kind of you." My mother said.

"I know you all must be tired from your journey. Acadia told us about the trouble you had once she arrived at your home." Queen Zadra took over the conversation. Where her husband's voice was loud and boisterous, hers' was soft and warm. "We have your rooms all ready for you to retire in for the evening."

"How gracious of you," my father said with a slight nod in the Queen's direction. "It has been a long trip."

"Acadia," the Queen spoke directly to her, her tone leaving no room for discussion. "We will speak once your family has retired to their rooms."

"Yes, your highness." She bowed slightly, and the Royal Family turned and left without another word.

"Follow me." A meek voice spoke up from the left. We turned to see a young woman no older than me standing there. She was wearing a long tan dress that covered her from her neck to the bottom of her toes.

My mother nodded, the young woman turned, and we followed her to the castle entrance.

I tried to hide the shocked expression on my face but castles on Earth, not that I visited them much on Earth, had nothing on this castle.

I couldn't find the words in to describe it, but my father did. "It's beautiful."

"The castle was built many years ago by our first queen, Queen Sree Nur. King Ezir's distant ancestor. It has been updated multiple times to fit the taste of the ruling family of the time. King Ezir has yet to change the castle; he has allowed it to reflect the tastes of his father." Our guide informed us, well us meaning my father and me. I'm sure my mother already knew the history.

Our guide took us down a long hallway and up two floors on an elevator. But the elevator wasn't the kind that I was used to - it was just a platform that we stood on that lifted us to the fifth floor. I mean, I thought we were on the fifth floor; it moved so fast I wasn't sure.

The first door we came to was large, black, and looked like it was made of marble, but the texture was different. I made a mental note to ask Vikram about it later.

"This will be Abriana's room." The guide said as she gave the door a slight push. The great door heaved open with little resistance, and I walked in.

"This is my room?" I stared in awe at the sheer size. "It's bigger than the entire second floor of our house."

"Don't lie," my dad laughed taking in the room for himself. "This room is larger than our entire home."

"If you will sir," the lady said from the door. "Your room is down the hall."

My dad turned to me. "Will you be alright?"

I nodded, and my dad smiled.

"Vikram, you will stay with her," my Mother said motioning to him. I never noticed Vikram walking behind us. My father walked over to my mother. She reached out a hand, and he took it. I watched her smile as she guided them down the hall.

Chapter Seven

After we were shown to my room, Vikram told me to change so we could go to the gym.

I found myself in weirdest, but the most state of the art, the gym I had ever seen. The room was littered with the equipment I never heard of or even seen, but Vikram assured me that they each piece was necessary. I had wanted to relax from the day the flight and the landing but the athlete in me was in awe of the gym I felt my body buzz with a second wind.

Vikram had me running on a treadmill for the past thirty minutes and I wanted to die. My legs burned with pain, and I was ready to stop for the day. I knew I missed running but I didn't remember it being this hard. I sighed and placed my legs on either side of mat.

"Giving up already?" Prince Nasol voice startled me as he walked in and leaning against the wall.

"Excuse me?" I panted, trying to catch up my breath.

"I asked are you giving up already? It looks like you have only run a mile." He motioned towards the treadmill's display.

"I've actually ran three but seeing as I was blown up a few weeks ago, I think I'm doing pretty well." I pressed the stop button and grabbed my water bottle from the holder on the treadmill. I took my time drinking my water, hoping that the prince would end his interrogation.

"Hmm," he said as he walked further in the gym. He passed Vikram and me without another word and headed towards the back of the gym. He disappeared behind a black door I hadn't noticed before.

"What's back there?" I whispered to Vikram.

"Another training room, there are simulators for more realistic training. It is for when hand to hand combat might be too risky."

"As in?" I pushed.

"Nasol is the crown prince of this kingdom. Normal combat is fine, but with weapons, it is not always safe to fight.

With the simulation room, Nasol can practice with close combat, and the guards do not have to worry about seriously injuring him."

"Oh," I said as I stepped off the treadmill. My legs were starting to feel like jelly.

"No," Vikram grabbed my arm and lifted me back up. "We are not done."

I groaned and stepped back on the treadmill. "How much longer?"

"How about until I stop," Vikram said getting on the treadmill next to me.

"No!" I crossed my arms in protest. "You're just starting. I already ran three miles."

"You need to get the use of your legs back to normal. I will not push you too far, but you and I both know you can do better so you are not done for the day yet."

"Vikram!" I whined hating how I sounded, but he shook his head turned on his treadmill.

"The more you whine, the longer I will run." He chuckled at me, and I narrowed my eyes at him, but he turned his head from me and focused on running.

I wanted to throw a tantrum. I was tired, I was on a new planet and all I wanted was a long bath followed by a nap. But instead, I started to run along side him.

I focused on my breathing and the movement of my legs. I could do this. I used to run all the time back on Earth, but it was different here.

My legs were different.

They sucked.

We ran silently next to each other, the only sound we could hear was the sound of our breathing and our feet pounding on the treadmill. Finally, after thirty minutes and two more miles, Vikram started to slow down.

I let out an internal squeal of joy and started to slow down as well, but he kept at this pace longer than I thought he would.

"He can run for an hour straight at that pace." I jumped at the sudden sound of Prince Nasol's voice. I lost my footing, tripped over my feet, and the speed and force of the treadmill sent me flying back, hard.

"Are you serious?" I screamed as I rolled over to my knees. I sat there trying to figure out how he got so close to me without my noticing. I didn't even hear him leave the simulation room. Vikram jumped off his treadmill and came over to help me up while Prince Nasol laughed silently.

"Wear a freaking bell!" I yelled at him, stretching my arm out.

"Why would I wear a bell?" Prince Nasol laughed. "It is not my fault you were not aware of your surroundings.

Vikram nodded in my direction once I exited the simulation room."

I stomped over to him. "Well, I'm not Vikram!" I poked his chest. He looked down at my finger and raised an eyebrow at me. With a swiftness, I didn't know was possible, Nasol snatched my hand and turned me around as he twisted my arm behind my back. He wasn't hurting me, but it was an uncomfortable hold.

"Nasol!" Vikram started, but Prince Nasol held up his free hand stopping him.

I felt Prince Nasol lean down close to my ear. "It seems you need to work on more than just your awareness. Your defenses are pathetic," he sneered. He pushed me away from him and released me from his grip. I stumbled forward, and Vikram caught me before I hit the ground.

"You need to train her in hand to hand combat." Prince Nasol said to Vikram before walking out of the gym, leaving us alone once more. I felt my face heat up with embarrassment and anger at his actions. How dare he!

"What is his deal?" I asked stretching out my arm.

"Prince Nasol would like you to improve," Vikram said still watching the empty doorway.

"Why does he care?"

"That, I do not know, yet" Vikram answered still watching the empty doorway. "But we will do what he has asked. Tomorrow you start your training."

"I'm already in training!" I protested.

"No, tomorrow you will start training in hand to hand combat."

"Why? Just because he suggested it to you!"

"That was not a suggestion; he was ordering me to train you." He said.

"I don't understand." I shook my head. "Why would he care?"

Vikram shrugged, the first time I saw him shrug. "He does not have to explain himself to me. If he orders, I will obey."

I rolled my eyes. "Well I don't have to, he's not my prince."

"While you are on this planet, he is your prince, and you will do as he says."

"Seriously!" I huffed. "Don't I have a say in my own life?"

"There is no point in complaining," Vikram said. "We will start bright and early for your training."

Chapter Eight

"Dad this is not funny!" I yelled.

My father sat across from me in my room. We were having a quiet dinner together while my mother met with the King to discuss the attack at our home. Not that we could be a part of it, much to me and my father's annoyance.

Granted, it was nice to admit that a woman did have one of the highest jobs in this world. After my training with Vikram tomorrow, I was to start my private lesson with a tutor to learn more about the planet's history.

When I asked my father about it, he only told me he was going to start studying about the history of the planet as well, but currently, we were talking about my extended training with Vikram.

"I'm sorry," my dad laughed. "But it is funny."

"It's not funny!" I repeated. "He was trying to kill me! I just got the use of my legs back, and he's killing them."

My dad nodded and put on a straight face. "Hun, I know this is hard for you, but it's what's best. You were a runner; your body is used to this. Or it will be soon. And the whole thing about hand to hand combat training, you must admit, it's not a bad thing to know. I do feel more comfortable with you knowing how to protect yourself while we are on this planet. I saw Vikram train while you were unconscious. He is a sight to see; you couldn't find a better teacher."

"But training just means we are going to be here longer. When can we go home?"

"I don't know Abriana. It could be a few weeks or a few months. Until your mother and her team find out who is behind this, it's safest if we stay here. Abriana," he walked over to me and cupped my face in my hands, "you almost died. I thought you were dead. They brought you back to me. I won't do anything that will put you in more danger." He kissed my forehead and pulled me into a tight hug.

"But I'm fine now Dad," I protested. He might've been on board with the plan to stay on this planet for as long as necessary, but I was not. I missed home.

"You weren't there. I saw your bones." He took a breath. "Abriana, I smelled your flesh burning. In any other situation, I would be standing over your grave. I am fine with any decision that keeps you alive." He whispered into my hair. "Take this training seriously. Please?"

I sighed and wrapped my arms around his waist and hugged him back. "Ok, fine," I said. "I will. And when I'm done, I'll be able to wipe the floor with Vikram."

I felt his laughter. "That's my girl."

"I'm sorry I don't mean to interrupt." I turned and saw her standing there. "I need to speak to you." She motioned for my father.

"Are you going to be fine on your own?" He asked releasing me.

I nodded but he didn't look convinced.

"You two talk," I said, and my father nodded and walked over to her.

"Abriana." She called, and I turned to face her. "I would like to sit down and talk, really talk, to you once everything gets a bit more under control."

I nodded, not trusting my voice to answer. Truth be told I wasn't sure if I was ready to speak with her. I was willing not to be hostile to her form my father's sake, but I still wasn't sure if I wanted to let her in.

They walked out of my room, and she left my door open slightly. I could have closed it but what would be the point? No one here really knocked on my door anyway. I would close it before I went to sleep.

I sighed as I walked over to my balcony. The view from my room was the private lake, and as it was getting darker, their pink moon reflected off the water beautifully.

I leaned against the railing and looked over the water thinking about how much my life had changed is such a few short days. Well, now it was more like a week, or weeks.

I wondered how my family back home felt at this moment. I knew they must've been worried sick if they still thought we were alive or utterly heartbroken if they thought we were dead. Either way, they were hurting.

"What are you doing out here?"

I jumped and turned around to see Prince Nasol standing behind me. "What is your problem?" I shrieked at him. "You can't sneak up on people like that."

"I am the crown prince of Elendil," he smirked at me. "I can do anything I want."

I took a breath and remembered Vikram's words that he was the Crown Prince of this world, but it still didn't give him the right to act like a jerk all the time. "You know you should be nicer to your guests, acting like a spoiled brat isn't a good look. I mean this is my first time here and all you've ever done is put me down. Do you have a problem with me?"

"What?" he asked, and I could tell he was surprised by my words.

I rolled my eyes, "I asked do you have a problem with me?"

He stared at me for a few seconds and I held his stare refusing to back down. Very slowly his lips curved up into a small smile. "You don't back down?"

"Not to bullies," I said.

He held my gaze a few seconds and asked another question. "What are you doing out here?" he finally asked.

"You know you could have asked that from the beginning instead being a jerk." I turned back to the lake. "But I'm taking in your planet. I'm admiring your lake and how the moon reflects off it."

"Why?" He asked as he stood next to me.

"It's beautiful." I sighed looking up at the moon. "Your moon is pink, and it reflects off the water in such a unique way. I've never seen anything like it before."

"Hmm," he said looking over at me.

"What?" I rolled my eyes. "You don't think it does?"

He shrugged. "It looks the same as it always has. I grew up here. The view never changes." He said, still staring at me.

"Why are you staring at me?" I asked turning away from the weight of his gaze.

"You're the first Earthling I have met face to face."

"And?" I pressed.

"I guess they are not all as beautiful as I have been led to believe."

"Excuse me?!" I whipped around to face him. "What is that supposed to mean? I literally just said you were being a jerk. What is wrong with you. Are you only able to express emotion if you are putting other people down?"

He held my glare for a moment then laughed. "You are too easy to rile up. You should work on that." He winked at me.

"Is that another order?" I wanted to shut his smug face up.

He gave me a slight nod.

"I'm not one of your subjects; you can't order me around. But that's beside the point, why are you so interested in how I act?"

"I'm always for the betterment of others." He answered. He should take himself up on his own word.

"Well, I don't need you to better me. I like the way I am." I said.

"It's not just you that you need to worry about. While you are here, you also represent your mother. You will be meeting many people while you stay here, you need to be as poised and as trained as she is."

"Who am I meeting that I haven't already met?" I asked. "I mean I already met your parents and they seemed to like me just fine. Why do I care how people who are beneath them think about me?"

He sighed. "I should not be telling you this, but we are hosting a gala in a few short days. You will meet some of the most important members of this world. Some of our closest allies will be here. You will want to make a good impression."

"What if I don't want to make a good impression?" I shot back. I didn't mean it; the words were out of my mouth before I could stop myself. I really needed to work on that. Crap, Nasol was already in my head.

"Don't be a child." He scolded. "You do not want to embarrass your father as well. It will reflect poorly on him if you act as if you have no training at all. Although you are your mother's child, your father is the one who raised you. You do not want people questioning his abilities. Now do you?"

I huffed and turned back to the grounds. I felt his gaze on me once more then he turned and walked back into my room. I let out a breath I didn't realize I was holding was once I heard my door close. What was his problem and why was it directed at me? What did I do to deserve his bullying?

Chapter Nine

"Again!" Vikram ordered.

I grimaced and picked myself off the ground and faced him again. "Can we take a break?" I pleaded. "We've been at this for days. I'm so sore."

"Stop complaining. You are improving fast. We will rest once you can deflect my attack." Vikram held up his hand again.

I groaned matching his stance. He was right; I was improving faster than I expected. From where I was a few days ago to now was nothing short of a miracle. But I had always healed quicker and obtained new skills faster than my peers growing up. As he said a few days ago, it was courtesy of my alien half.

"Go!" He yelled and came at me. I backed up once I saw his fist fly towards my head. "Do not run, deflect," he ordered.

I moved forward, tilted my hips, and raised my leg up to kick, but he brought up his forearm and stopped my foot connecting with his head.

"Good!" He praised and moved in for another attack.

We fought for another hour until I was drenched in sweat and could barely stand.

"We will stop, for now," Vikram finally said.

"Finally." I sighed dropping to the ground in a heap. "I'm just going to stay here…, forever." I yawned.

"Get up." He walked over to me and held out a hand.

"Fine." I sighed taking it. He hoisted me to my feet with one short pull.

"Use the tub," he ordered as he started packing up our equipment. I nodded and walked to the ladies' room on shaky feet. The 'tub' was more like a vat that I could sit in, and it was a godsend. It was like the one that saved my life after the explosion. Only this one was made for healing the body after a hard training session rather than one on the verge of death.

I didn't need to use it after every training session, but tonight's the night the castle was hosting a formal welcoming gala for myself and my father. I couldn't limp around the Gala with old and new bruises marring my body, and with only thirty minutes in the tub, I wouldn't have to.

I dragged myself to the bathroom and the tub in the back room. I struggled to pull off my pants and top because they were stuck to my skin. I programmed the container to the temperature and healing setting I needed. I stepped inside, sat down, and closed it around my neck only leaving my head exposed as the soaking tub filled up quickly with steaming hot water. I breathed out a sigh of relief and closed my eyes as the water warmed my body and started to heal me.

I relaxed as I felt the jets start up and thought about the last few days. I had started my first tutoring session with the castle historian about Elendil. To be frank, they have a long history. A long, long, history. We decided it was best to start with the most important items and fill in the rest later. After day one, I did learn about The Union of Plants with in the Isildur system. When I asked why they had a separate name, he told me not all planets in the system were apart of The Federation of Planets. There was more he said, but after the first three hours it all started to go over my head. I would have to review my notes before our next meeting. He just seemed like the type of guy to give pop quizzes. I should ask Vikram to help me study.

I took another deep breath cleared my mind and felt myself fall into a peaceful nap.

I was awakened by the sound of the vat beeping, indicating that my soak was over. I blinked and looked around waiting for the water to drain itself thoroughly. Once the final beep sounded the door opened, I rolled my neck and stood up.

I grabbed a towel, quickly dried off, and threw on my extra clothes. I picked up my dirty clothes and threw them in my gym bag.

Vikram was still in the gym when I walked out, but he wasn't alone; he was training with Prince Nasol. Seeing them spar, I realized how good he really was and how much he was holding back with me.

He and Prince Nasol were experts in the craft. The way they moved; I could tell they were used to fighting with each other. Their moves fed off one another but they were still aimed to hurt.

I didn't know if I should interrupt them or not, but given the level of their training, I knew they knew I was here. It looked like they weren't going to stop anytime soon, and I needed to get back to my room. I walked around the edge of the room so to not disturb them. I had just made it to the door when I heard his voice.

"Where are you going?" I turned back to face them, but they were still fighting, Vikram was talking to me.

"Back to my room," I answered. "I need to start getting ready for tonight."

Vikram never took his eyes off Prince Nasol, "You are not allowed to walk the halls alone. I will be done in a moment, and I will walk you back." He swiped his foot out sweeping at Prince Nasol's feet and knocked him on his back.

"Like hell," Prince Nasol grunted and flipped back up on to his feet. He landed a kick to Vikram's stomach, and when Vikram doubled over, Prince Nasol sent a knee to his face, sending Vikram sprawling on his back.

"Vikram!" I dropped my bag and ran over to him, his hands were cupped around his face, and I could see blood slipping out from between his fingers. "I can't believe you!" I screamed at Prince Nasol.

"He's fine." Prince Nasol waved his hand, dismissing my concern.

Vikram rolled over to his knees and stood up. "I am fine Abriana." He voice was muffled by his hands. "But I do need to have this taken care of."

"I'll go with you." I offered, but he shook his head no and shared a look with the prince.

"Prince Nasol can walk you back to your room since it is his fault, I am unable to do so now."

"What? No," I protested, as I glared at Prince Nasol. He was so… ugh, I couldn't think of the right word to describe him, but pushy close enough.

"It is my duty." Prince Nasol replied. He grabbed his towel and handed it over to Vikram who applied it to his face. "And take the next two days off, your face will need time to heal."

I looked at the two men. I wasn't quite sure what was going on, but I was sure I didn't understand the silent conversation happening between them.

"Yes, thank you." Vikram nodded his head.

"Come," Prince Nasol placed his hand on my lower back and turned me to the exit. "I'll escort you back to your room."

"Hey!" I swatted his hand away. "Just because you are a prince doesn't mean you can touch me!"

Prince Nasol rolled his eyes but thankfully kept his hands to himself. I glanced back at Vikram, but he had already left the room, probably to the bathroom.

"Why did you have to do that?" I asked once we were further down the hall. "I thought you were friends."

He chuckled. "We are friends, what I did was barely a scratch. It will be healed within the hour. Vikram has done much worst to me. I do believe last time we sparred I ended up with a broken cheekbone and a cracked rib. We fight to do damage."

"Why?"

"In a real fight, your opponent won't stop because you are injured. Fighting while injured only prepares us for a real fight."

I thought over his words. I guess it did make sense, but I didn't like it.

"We are here." Prince Nasol said as he opened my door. Three women were waiting in my room. I was told this morning they were going to be here to help me prepare for the Gala. "See you tonight." He winked and walked away. I rolled my eyes and turned back to the women and walked in.

"Hello, Abriana." The middle one nodded. "My name is Arka, and this is my team. Vala." The girl to her left nodded her head. "And this is Clara." The girl on her right nodded. "We are here to help you get ready. Your mother will also be here later to talk to you."

"To talk?" I asked.

"Yes, she will be here to speak to you before the Gala. Now, come, we have much to do."

"Oh, thanks," I said as they collectively escorted me into my bathroom.

Chapter Ten

"Oh, my stars." I exhaled as I turned in the mirror. The dress was beautiful; though technically it wasn't a dress, it was a top and skirt. The top had a high halter neckline with an open back. It was white silk fabric that stopped an inch above my belly button. The material was embroidered with gold and jewels that wrapped around my back to clasp together. The skirt portion of my dress started right at my belly button and flowed down like waves. I loved it! It fit my body perfectly. I wasn't sure if this was acceptable in my father's eyes, but I didn't care – the dress was beautiful.

"You look beautiful." I turned to see my mother standing in the doorway. She was also wearing a white dress, though hers was just one piece. She had a sweetheart neckline that had gold accents along the neckline. The dress fit her like a glove, and I was thankful mine wasn't that tight. I never got the hang of walking in those dresses.

"Hi." I nodded to her not sure of what I should say.

"May we have the room." It sounded like a question, but I knew it was an order. Arka, Vala, and Clara all bowed slightly and walked out of the room closing the door behind them. "Abriana…" She paused as if she was trying to find the right words. She walked over to the couch, sat down, and patted the empty space next to her. I walked over and sat down across from her. She grimaced but didn't say anything. "I know you are angry at me, and you have every right to be. I know I hurt you and your father more than I can ever imagine."

"Do you have any idea what you did to him? I was too young to realize it then, but my family let me know how much you hurt him."

She nodded. "I know, I felt it through our bond. But you have to know to leave you both was the hardest thing I have ever done."

"Bond?" I asked focusing on that word.

She smiled and touched a ring on her right hand, I never noticed it before, it was silver and blue metal wrapped together.

"Dad has the same ring," I said.

She smiled. "They are bond rings; I gave your father his before I left. Your father is my mate, the only man I will ever love."

"Vikram told me," I said.

"Abriana, I want a relationship between us, and I know it will not happen overnight. I know I need to earn your trust, but I want you to know I am not going anywhere ever again."

"What happens when we go back to Earth?" I asked testing the waters.

"If that is your wish, I will go with you. I've spoken to the king, and he is prepared to have me replaced so I can be with you both."

"Dad said he didn't know when we could go back. Do you?"

"No, the attack at your house proves we still have enemies out there. We thought the war was over, but it seems we are not as at peace as we thought. Once we are sure we are no longer at risk, I will follow you both anywhere."

"Knock, knock." We looked towards the door. My father stood there and, like us, he was wearing a white suit. But his suit wasn't the same color as ours; his was a shade darker.

"Hey, Dad," I smiled.

"What's going on in here?" He looked between us.

"We were just talking." I stood up. My dad crossed the room but stopped once he got a full view of my dress.

"Where is the rest of you dress?"

"What are you talking about?" I asked looking down, trying to hide my smile.

"No," he shook his head. "That is not the dress you are wearing tonight. You are going to change. Now."

"I don't have anything else to change into." I looked at her for backup.

"Brenden, I picked out the dress for her," she replied as she stood up.

"And I repeat, where is the rest of it? Look at her! I can see her skin," he sputtered.

"She looks fine; she is beautiful!"

"No," he said, shaking his head, "she's changing. I'm not blind I see the way the prince looks at her. She is not going out there looking like that."

"Wait," I interrupted, a bit amused and bit disgusted. "What are you talking about? How does Prince Nasol look at me?"

"Don't worry about it." My dad growled. "But you are not wearing that dress!"

"It's a perfectly normal dress here Brenden." My mother defended. "I had it made just for her," she turned to face me with a smile, "and I think she looks beautiful in it."

"I see her skin!" He all but yelled in return. "I won't allow it," he fumed.

"Brenden please," she nearly begged. "I would not have her dressed in a way that disgraces her or us."

My dad looked between the two of us and sighed. "I don't like the two of you doing this." His frown turned into a smile. "This ganging up on me thing. I don't like it."

"Well, I never had the chance to try it before." I smiled at him.

"Fine. But if I see anyone look at her differently, I'm taking her out of there."

"I will agree to that." She nodded.

"Thanks, Dad." I beamed as I hugged him.

"Well, let's go." He said as he opened the door for us. I walked out first, and they followed me, their arms linked behind me.

Chapter Eleven

We walked through the castle, together as a family, until we reached the doors of the Great Hall.

I could hear the music and various voices emanating from the other side.

"Are you ready?" She asked as I stopped at the doors.

"Your father and I will enter first and then you will come behind us."

I nodded and stood behind them. She leaned forward and gave the door a slight knock and stepped back.

The door swept open, and the entire hall turned to face us. I could see that the room was filled with at least a hundred people. All different shapes, colors, and sizes. I could even see a few aliens who were not so human like.

My mother took a slight step forward, my father followed and stood next to her as a voice boomed overhead.

"I introduce to you, General Arcadia and her mate, Brenden, of Earth." The crowd clapped as they walked forward. "And their daughter Abriana." I took a breath and stepped forward into the room. I swept my eyes over the place again and immediately met Prince Nasol's eyes. He was standing in the corner surrounded by a few people I had yet to meet during my time in the castle. But he looked very cozy with them, most of the females seemed to be hanging on his every word. They looked to be around his age. His eyes swept over my dress, and his face hardened as I saw his grip on his drink tighten.

Panic filled my body and I felt my blood rush to my face; did he think I looked horrible? Was my father correct? Was this dress completely inappropriate? I subconsciously ran my hand down my torso and did a once over of my outfit. Checking out my angles slowly as to not draw to my attention to myself.

"Welcome!" King Ezir's voice swept over us as he and the Queen walked towards us.

"Thank you, your Grace." My father reached out and shook his hand. The Queen came forward and kissed my mother's cheek. She walked over to me and kissed my cheek as well.

"You look beautiful." The Queen gushed holding me out at arm's length. "Almost like a princess." She winked and squeezed my hands before letting me go. Before I could dwell on her words, a line of aliens alike came up behind her to meet and greet us.

By the time the introductions were over I had met the ambassadors from Serkis, a planet full of water shaped blobs; ambassadors from Azlan, they were tall tree-like creatures; and the ambassadors from Florian, they were short, plump humanoid aliens with eyes that took up half of their face and a small mouth. My mother discreetly explained they observe more than they ever talk, which came in handy during times of conflict or when they counseled others.

I went on to meet ambassadors from Xiaatana, Crao 4, and about twenty more planets and territories that I would never remember. I also met some of the essential members of the ruling council on Elendil. I made sure to control my breathing, it was all a bit, no that's a lie, it was completely overwhelming. I felt my heart race at the thought of all the people, aliens in the room. That I was in the room with them and I was part alien. I quickly closed my eyes and counted to ten in my head and let out a breath as I felt my heart slow back down to its normal beat.

I was first introduced to the general right under my mother. He and his wife were beautiful people both were tall with deep chocolate complexion. Paolo the General had almond shaped eyes while his wife Colette had wide purple eyes that were full of laughter and mirth. Their children were currently off-planet in school studying on their mother's home planet, but I never got the name of that world. I would have to remember to ask my mother later.

I met the King's closest adviser Becix. He was a short man; he barely came to my shoulder. He had a wide face with sunken eyes. He was polite enough, but I could tell he was only tolerating me for the sake of my mother. He gave off this air of superiority that didn't sit right with me. I was also warned by Virkam that not everyone, mostly Becix, was happy about the arrival of my father and me. He apparently advised the King against allowing her to come get us from earth, but when I tried to get more info, Vikram wouldn't answer. I made a mental note to ask him about it later.

I then met a few other advisors for different aspects of the planet, but it happened so quickly I forgot their name as soon as they mentioned it. Finally, I was able to go and mingle.

I walked around the gala, nodding and smiling at everyone who caught my eye. Every few minutes someone else would stop me to ask questions about our life on Earth. I was told to keep my answers short and to the point. I let them know that I was in high school and ran track, and that my dad was a doctor. Plus, I wasn't sure if they were asking for the right reasons to begin with.

"Abriana." I turned and saw Prince Nasol walking to toward me, carrying two glasses of clear liquid. "Are you enjoying your evening?" He asked, handing one of the glasses to me.

"I am. It's going well," I said unsure of how to answer, I took a sip of the drink. The drink was bubbly and tickled my nose. It was light on my tongue and had a slight lemony taste, but overall it wasn't that bad.

"Let's step outside." Prince Nasol said as he motioned towards the terrace. He placed his hand on my lower back, and I felt a slight tingle at his touch. I ignored the feeling and allowed him to continue to guide me onto the terrace, if only to get away from the large crowd for a few moments.

"My parents are talking to yours; you know." He said once we were out of earshot of everyone else.

"About what?" I asked. He led us over to the far side where there were no windows for people to see us talking.

"They are talking about us," he said taking a sip of his drink.

"I don't understand," I said.

"Does 'us' mean something different on your planet?"

"No 'us' in this context would mean you and I. But I was asking why they would be talking about us?"

"I am of mating age, as are you."

"Excuse me?" I turned to face him, nearly dropping my glass. "Mating like marriage?"

He nodded. "I have not found a mate yet, and here you are, dropped in our lap. You come from good stock, and you are not bad to look at. Also, my father and your mother are very close friends; they will love this."

I laughed at the absurd thought. "That is the biggest load of bull I have ever heard."

"You do not want to mate with a prince?" He asked, slightly taken aback.

"No!" I hissed. "I just met you like four days ago, and I'm only seventeen. I'm not old enough to mate even if I wanted to, and I don't," I quickly added on the end. "You do get how weird you are being right? Like is it normal for people on your planet to act like this? "

"Mating age is when you have had your first cycle, don't most girls have their cycles by now?"

"I am not listening to this." I shook my head. "You're crazy and besides Vikram already told me how the mating thing works, enough for me to know that you are lying."

He stared at me and I stared back until a smile spread across his face, which was quickly followed by laughter.

"What's so funny?" I asked staring at him.

"Fine you've gotten me. I'm joking." He laughed. "I just wanted to see your reaction. I should be offended. I thought most girls from Earth wanted to marry a prince."

"I'm not most girls, and you've been nothing but a horrible rude jerk to me since I've gotten here. Telling me I would be stuck with you forever doesn't bode well with me."

He just shook his head at my explanation and turned his attention down to the valley.

"What are looking at?" I asked more annoyed than ever that my feelings were being ignored again by him, but why did I care?

"My favorite view." He said then turned back to me. "So, you don't want to mate with me?"

I rolled my eyes at his statement. "Seriously is that all you heard? Do you have a complex where you want all women to want you? When I walked into the gala, you were surrounded by plenty of girls who looked like they would love the chance to be your mate. Though, let's be honest why would I, and I repeat, since meeting me you have belittled me, scared me, you broke Vikram's nose just to show me you could. If you were really a great prince, you would have realized I've just had my entire life turn upside down in a way I never thought possible. That I'm on a planet I never knew existed with a mother who I thought didn't give a crap about me my father since I was a baby. That maybe I'm going through a lot right and maybe you could try to be nice but no, that's too much to ask. Basically, you've been a school yard bully to me just for your princely amusement. Why would being your mate ever sound good to me right now?"

"So, you're the jealous type? I can work with that." He smirked.

I closed my eyes feeling rage fill me, is that really all he took from that? That I was the jealous type? He wasn't worth a response. Instead I turned to go back to the gala, but his hand shot out and grabbed mine stopping me from walking away.

"Let go." I said not turning to face him. "I'm pretty sure my father will realize I'm missing."

"I'm sorry Abriana." He said, and for the first time since meeting him his voice didn't sound like he was joking.

"You're what?" I repeated turning to face him against my better judgement. He was looking down at our joined hands then looked up at me.

"You are right, I have been a jerk, a bully and I am sorry. I thought it would come off as a joke, like in one of your old American movies about your high schools. I did not intend to hurt your feelings. This is a tough time for you, and I have not made your first days here pleasant. I am sorry, but I can say, your responses to my actions has shown your father raised a very strong young woman and that is a credit to you both. If I may, can I ask if we can start over."

I mulled over my answer for a few seconds, on the one hand, he did look and sound sincere, but the petty side of me wanted to lash back out, but I was going to be here a while, whether I liked it or not. Life could go easier if we were at least friends. " I accept your apology." I finally said and to lighten the mood I continued but pulled my hand from his, "and you know if you wanted to know the type of woman my father raised you just had to ask?"

He gave me a little laugh. "I was thinking I would figure you out in my own way."

"So, entitled." I faked glared at him.

"I'm a prince." He retorted winking at me.

"Yes," I rolled my eyes. "You are 'Prince Nasol.'"

He chuckled and looked back out at the dark grounds. "Just call me Nasol, you don't have to call me Prince."

"I don't get it. Your favorite view is darkness?" revering back to his earlier statement and trying to change the subject.

"Just give it a minute." He said looking on.

I looked over the darkness and sighed, waiting for whatever was supposed to come.

Then it happened.

Orbs of light began to rise up and fill the night sky. Its kind of reminded me of fireworks, but unlike the fireworks back home, the orbs floated, moved, changed colors, and shifted into different shapes.

"I don't understand," I said, completely in awe of the light show that unfolded before me.

"That valley is full of light mages. A few years ago, due to the destruction from multiple civil wars they were almost wiped out on their home planet. By the end of the last war, the planet was all but dead. No life could be sustained for much longer. My father felt for them as we had just finished our war and life was becoming semi normal, reached out and offered some of the survivor part of our land for them live on, this way most families and towns could stay together. I believe my father acted as he did because if our war did not end as it did, he would have wished someone would have stepped in and helped his people. They have come a long way in the few years they have been here, and thankfully a few other planets reached out and helped other townships, so their numbers are finally growing once more.

Now, every time we have an event, as a way of thanking us, they give us a little light show. I've never seen the same show twice."

"Wow," I exhaled taking in the sight. "Oh," I gasped as I saw my face, well, the outline but I could clearly tell it was me, in the sky.

"I told them you were here," he explained. "With your father being the mate of the general and you her daughter, they wanted you to feel welcome."

"It's beautiful!" I gushed looking at the lights. "They must be really grateful."

"They are. Right now, my father is working with their leader to help them find a new planet to move to."

"They can't stay here forever?" I asked.

"Well, they could, but they don't want to," he said as another wave of orbs began to rise and change colors. "When they came here, my father offered them the land forever, but they only wanted it for five years maximum. They wanted to find somewhere that was theirs where all the survivors can move to start over and rebuild."

A breeze swept around us causing a shiver up my spine.

"Are you cold?" He asked taking a step closer to me. I felt his body heat warming me slightly.

"Just a bit, we should head back inside," I said taking a step back from him.

He held out an arm, and I took it. We started back towards the party when, for the second time in my life, the air exploded around me.

Chapter Twelve

I flew back hard. My body was hurled over the terrace, down the hill, and I rolled for several feet until I came to a stop. I closed my eyes and covered my ears with my hands trying to block out the pounding in my skull. When I opened them again my vision blurred, and I felt something warm slide down the side of my face. I reached up and touched my face and tried to focus on my hand but closed my eyes once more.

'Breath Abriana, breath' I repeated in my head trying to calm myself down and focus. I opened my eyes once more and looked at my hand again, my focus was getting better, and I could see it was my blood. I was bleeding.

I took another breath and smelled wood burning and heard the crackling of flames above me, but the trees that surrounded me were fine. I pushed myself up on the heels of my hands and looked around. I felt my world come it to focus as the small sounds of a crackling fire was replaced with screams and the roar of flames.

I looked around and saw Nasol lying a few feet away from me, sprawled on his back with a gash on his forehead and bright blue blood running down the side of his face.

"Nasol!" I screamed, but over the roaring fire, he couldn't hear me. I struggled to my knees and tried to stand but my body couldn't take it and fell back down. I shook my head trying to get my bearing but opted to crawl over to him. "Nasol!" I screamed again once I reached him, giving him a shake. "Nasol wake up." I basically pleaded, he couldn't be dead, he just couldn't. How was I going to explain this?

I shook him a few more times until I heard him groan and I let out a sigh of relief. He wasn't dead.

Another explosion rocked the castle grounds; I felt the land under my body and the trees around us shake with the force. I ducked covering Nasol with my body as chucks of the castle rained down around us. I risked a look up and saw the tips of the trees surrounding us were alight with fire.

That one was more powerful than the first

I looked back at Nasol and gave him another shake until he finally came to.

"Wha-" he groaned blinking up at me. "What happened-" He tried to sit up, but he immediately fell back down to the ground. He struggled a few more times and was finally able to sit upright.

"There was an explosion, I don't know from where," I answered, "I think something in the castle exploded."

His shook his head as he was trying to focus, on my words or the situation I wasn't sure. "My parents!" He yelled finally pushing himself to his feet. He swayed slightly but was able to remain upright. "Stay here." He ordered. "I'll be right back." He made his way up the hill and headed back up to the castle.

I tried to stand up, but I couldn't stop my head from spinning. I waited, my heart hammering in my chest, for Nasol to return. I closed my eyes and felt my chest tighten; I couldn't have a panic attack here. I counted to ten as slow as I could forcing myself to relax as much as I could. Once I felt I was more in control a few minutes later I opened my eyes once more.

On top of the hill I could see the glow of the flames, and down in the valley, I saw more and more lights turn on but a few seconds later, Nasol came running down the hill.

"What-" Before I could finish my question, he scooped me up and started running. "What-" I tried again.

"Shh." He hissed, taking us around the trees just as shots rang out. I gripped him tighter as he carried us further in the darkness. I held on to him as tight as I could, last thing I needed was for him to drop me, and I guess he didn't think I could run to where ever he was taking us. He ran carrying me for another ten minutes until we came to a small opening. He gently placed me down, pulled up a little latch, grabbed me again, and together we dropped into the darkness. He gently placed me down again and then reached up closing the opening.

"Nasol." I whispered, but he covered my mouth, his silent way of telling me to stay quiet. Soon after, I heard the sound of thundering footsteps and shouts above us. I looked at the ceiling waiting for the voices and steps to die down.

I wanted to speak again, Nasol's still covered my mouth. We sat there in silence for what felt like an eternity while my heart hammered in my chest before he finally spoke.

"We've been attacked," he said. His voice hard, his face fixed.

"What do you mean?"

"Everything I could see was destroyed. I was barley up there before I was being shot at."

"Who shot at you, it must be chaotic up there, and everyone is on their guard. Are you sure they knew it was you? Maybe they thought you were someone else, someone attacking." I reasoned, it had to be a mistake.

He shook his head. "I know one of the guards who was firing at me. I didn't recognize the others, but the one I did, he has known me since I was a child. I was close enough for him to see me clearly, he still fired. We are undergoing a coup."

"A coup?" I could barely whisper the words.

He spat on the ground. "I do not want to believe it. But we should have expected something after what happened at your house."

"What about our parents?"

He shook his head. "If they are lucky, they're dead."

"Don't say that." I cried.

He shook his head. "If they are alive, they will be tortured then killed."

"Why would a coup happen now? I thought everything was settled here?"

"So, did we," he sighed. "Or at least we allowed ourselves to become lax in our thinking. I thought we would finally live in peace. We believed the war was truly over, and we have allowed ourselves to become a target once more."

"You mean the war that brought my mother back here?" I asked. "I never did ask, what started it in the first place, we hadn't reached it yet in the turtoring."

"When the first Queen of Elendil ruled, she ruled over one kingdom, the entire planet. But after a few centuries, we separated into two kingdoms - the north and the south. The threat of civil war was what caused us to separate. The southern kingdom never liked that our allies favored the north more and that we prospered faster as a result. They felt they were the better people and so, ten years ago, they decided they wanted to rule over all the planet once again, and they attacked us. It took years for the trust to resume. This was the first year without an incident, well, until tonight. We thought we were finally living in peace. But I was wrong. We were wrong." He shook his head. "They must have been planning this for years. To get this close to the castle, to my home, to my family, to destroy it all. To take it over like this." He banged is fist on the nearby wall.

"What do we do next?"

"We fight. I will lead my people in the fight to take back the Kingdom."

"And how do you know who to trust?" I asked. "I mean, you said a guard you've known your entire life just tried to kill you. Who can you trust?"

He paused and rubbed his face with his hands. "I do not know." He said. "I first need to see how far the damage has spread. Once it's safe, we will go topside and get to the closest house and find out what has happened."

"Is that wise?"

"I am not hiding when my nation is under attack. It is my duty as crown prince to protect my people."

"I'll come with you; it's my father they attacked as well," I said desperately wishing it wasn't so. Desperately wishing that this wasn't my reality. That I wasn't in some dark pit pondering the mortality of my parents.

It was a long night. I slept for maybe an hour before Nasol woke me up. Slowly and cautiously, we made our way out the opening and back into the world.

I swallowed my gasp at the scene before me. The forest was burnt and covered with scorch marks from the weapon fire.

Nasol grabbed my hand and pulled me, quickly but quietly, through the forest. Luckily, we didn't run into anyone until we got closer to town.

As we walked through a small clearing, I made sure to keep close to Nasol. The last thing I needed was to get separated from him. Not now.

We were swiftly making our way across the clearing when a guard stumbled out of the woods across from us. We slowed to a stop as he righted himself. "Damn undergrowth." He mumbled before looking up and spotting us.

"Hey!" He screamed lifting his gun towards us. "Freeze," he shouted, but Nasol was faster.

I dropped to the ground as the guard started firing towards us. Nasol dodged the next round of shots and swiftly made contact with the guard. He grabbed the gun and slammed his head into the guard's neck.

The guard wheezed, dropping his gun as he grabbed for his neck. Nasol grabbed the guard's head, turning him around and forcing him to his knees. And, with one smooth move, Nasol snapped the guard's neck. I swallowed hard as Nasol dropped the guard's body to the ground.

He looked at me, "I need to move the body. Otherwise, others might find it."

Nasol grabbed the guard's legs and started to drag him back into the woods. He came back a few seconds later, took the guard's gun, and threw it over his shoulder. He held out his hand for mine, I placed my hand in his, and we kept going. Finally, we broke through another set of trees to another small clearing where a few houses sat dark in a small cul-de-sac neighborhood. Nasol glanced between a few of them and ran to the house furthest from us. We ran around back, and Nasol pressed on a panel near the door, and a keypad appeared. He pressed a few buttons, and the door to our left quickly opened. Nasol entered first and pulled me in after him.

He wandered around the darkness with an ease that told me he had been there before. He pulled me into a room with large glass windows, walked over the window, and pressed his hand to the right. I guess there was a button there because a shade came down blocking our view of outside.

"Lights on." He said, finally breaking the silence. Light flooded the room, and I saw we were in a living room of sorts.

He walked over to the - I guess you could call it a TV, I mean that's what it looked like, and turned it on. He flipped through the channels until he found a news report. The attack was the top story, but what was on the screen seemed to be more of a script than an actual news report. The man on screen sat behind the standard news desk. However, he wasn't your typical reporter. Dressed in military garb the man proceeded to read his scripted lines:

"I am pleased to report this evening that peace will finally reign through the great lands of Elendil once again. The tyrannical rule of the North has been brought to a swift and necessary end. Both halves of this great nation – the North and the South – are no longer separate and are finally equals."

The man nodded, and the screen went momentarily blank before a video started playing.

"That bastard." Nasol hissed once a new face appeared on the screen.

"What?"

"He's supposed to be dead," Nasol screamed as he pointed at the screen.

"Who?"

"Borran, the one who is speaking. He is, well was, the prince of the South. They said he died in battle ten years ago, but it looks as if he just went underground once he knew they were going to lose the war. Coward. He must have planted people around us to spy and to wait until we were no longer on guard."

"Then why not attack when your general was off planet getting us?"

"He did, remember? Your house was blown up. We should have investigated it more. For them to go that far, we should have acted faster, interrogated harder, found the spies sooner."

We watched the screen as they replayed the explosion at the castle over and over in a loop. "Nasol." I placed a hand on his shoulder.

"He will pay for this. I will kill him for this. I will kill him with my bare hands!"

Chapter Thirteen

All regular programming was canceled, and the manifesto played on repeat a few times more times before a live stream filled the screen. Nasol sat up straighter as the ruined castle came into view. The flames were replaced with smoldering bunches of rocks. I gasped seeing the remains of charred bodies thrown about. The shot panned out, and the supposed dead prince Borran walked on screen flanked by a few men.

"This is a glorious day for all of Elendil," he started. "Today marks the beginning of the new regime. We have taken our world back from the corrupt rulers and today marks the beginning of the south becoming equal to the north. For us to be one family – one Elendil."

"We were always equal," Nasol growled under his breath.

Borran began again. "No longer will you have to live under the rule of a tyrannical leader who is unwilling to help his citizens." The men behind him shook their heads in agreement. "I have seen to the death of the royal family and their Head Generals, and I have destroyed their major bases and cities for your own protection. My men will start doing checks of the nation and anyone who is found loyal to the old ways, those who refuse to swear their allegiance to me will be killed along with their offspring and mates. I will not allow anyone who is against the true unification of our planet to live. Daily checks will begin today of every home on the planet. We will create a new police force to help us at this time."

I gasped after hearing his words. "He couldn't mean killing everyone who disagrees with him, could he? That just seems wrong."

"It's what he knows," Nasol said. "The south ruled that way. Under us, they were free. Now he wants to shove them all under his thumb. It's barbaric."

"Do you think the people will fight back?" I asked.

He shrugged. "Not without a leader. He killed the generals who would have supported my father, supported me. But..." A thought must have occurred to him because he lit up. "Vikram's off planet!"

"Vikram's alive?" Hope filled me at this revelation. My friend was still alive.

"Yes," he nodded. "I gave him two days off after I broke his nose and I believe he went off the planet. If I can get in contact with him, he can come to pick us up, and we can get out of here."

"*You're* going to leave your people?" I asked in disbelief.

"Don't look at me like that. I need support. The kind of support that I will not find here. I need an army to fight an army."

"Your people can be your army," I argued.

"I will not lead them to their deaths. The army is in shambles, and I need more to save them. I do not plan to leave them for long."

"But they need you, they need to know you are alive."

"It is best if they did not, at least at this time. If there were any whispers about my being alive, Borran would burn this whole planet to the ground to find me. I will not put my people through that. Besides, my absence will only be temporary."

"Your people didn't sign up to be left behind."

"You think this is the choice I want to make? This is the only option available to me now. Any allies we have are either in hiding, actively being hunted, or they are dead." He fumed as he turned away from me. "No citizen ever signs up for war, yet it is a possibility they are all faced with."

"But they are defenseless."

"I did *not* start this! The only choice I see right now is to get off the planet, regroup, and form a plan. Borran will have the support of the South, and they have always outnumbered us. We've just had the more advanced tech and weaponry. In a fight with just civilians, my people will be killed. I would rather leave, regroup and come back with a plan to save them." He shook his head. "I need a way to get in contact with Vikram. It will be best if we can get off the planet while we still can; while they still think that we are dead." He nodded at the screen as the image of the burned bodies reappeared.

I swallowed hard and nodded my head in agreement. I didn't know what to do in this situation, but I did know that I would follow Nasol wherever he went. I had to stick with him.

But damn, I was a long way from Earth, and all I wanted to do was go home.

Nasol started looking around the house for whatever he could use to contact Vikram. "Damn! No communicator." He said after a moment. "We might have to break into another house."

"You say it so casually," I said as I sat down on the couch. "Well, when are we leaving?" I asked, finally resigning myself to the travel this road of criminal activity we were on. "I don't think it will be a problem, breaking in again. Though will it be a problem if someone is there. I mean what if they aren't loyal to you?"

He shook his head. "It would be best if you stay hidden until I get what we need to get off the planet. It is safer for you to stay here. I know this area better."

"Why can't I stay with you?" I asked not entirely trusting that he wouldn't leave me the moment he got the chance to. This was his planet after all. I was not one of his people; he didn't have to worry about me. Plus, he was the only person I knew left on this planet. I couldn't...

"Cut that out!" He said, his hardened voice breaking through my thoughts.

"Cut what out?" I asked.

"That doubt, I am not leaving you. Your mother has done so much for my family; I would never betray her like that." He paused as if trying to find the right words. "Abriana, it is my duty to protect you."

"Oh," I sunk deeper into the couch, feeling a bit embarrassed. "I'm sorry, but I did just meet you a few days ago."

"I respected your mother. I would never allow anything to happen to you while you are in my care. Where I go, you go…, after I get what we need to get off the planet. Right now, you will stay here and stay safe."

"Well, where do I hide? What if the people who live here come back."?

"They won't," he said quietly.

"How do you know?" I asked almost afraid of the answer.

He sighed heavily. "The castle cook lives…lived here. He was in the castle at the time of the attack. There is a good chance he will not be coming back."

"Maybe he made it out?" I said.

Nasol shook his head. "Even if he did, he was loyal to my father, to me. He wouldn't be kept alive. Right now, Borran and his supporters think we are dead, and that's a plus. We can lay low here until Vikram can get us off the planet."

I nodded in agreement with him, "OK."

He motioned to the TV. "While this is playing, they will be distracted. Their primary focus will be on trying to get the rioting under control. I can use this time to get what I need. While I'm gone, do not leave the house or raise the blinds. They block out all light; no one will be able to tell that you are here." He said grabbing a piece of clothing out of the side closet. Nasol left the room for a few minutes and came back dressed all in black. "Ok, I'll be back in a bit." He turned to look at me. His eyes lingered a bit longer than I expected and then it dawned on me that I must've looked like crap compared to how I looked at the beginning of the night. Nasol let out a sigh and left out the back door.

I sighed and slid back down on the couch and closed my eyes and cried as the weight of my present reality finally hit me. My father was dead - gone - and he was never coming back. How was I supposed to deal with this? I was only seventeen. I wasn't supposed to be dealing with this. I laid down on the couch, scooped up the nearest pillow, buried my face in it and screamed as loud and as hard as I could.

This wasn't fair.

He shouldn't be dead.

She shouldn't be dead!

My chest tightened as I screamed again and again and again until my throat was hoarse, and my eyes started to close. I spent my last moments of consciousness haggling with the Universe to reverse the last few weeks… and bring my family back. I was finally getting the family I always wanted, and now I was left with nothing.

Chapter Fourteen

I woke up to the voices on the television. I blinked a few times trying to clear my vision. The crust in my eyes indicated that I cried myself to sleep.

'How long was I out for?' I wondered.

"Nasol?" I called softly and waited, but there was no response. I sat up and stretched, shaking the thoughts that threatened to break me again from my head.

I looked around for the time - I had been asleep for just under five hours.

"Nasol!" I called a little louder this time and still no answer. Where was he? I jumped to my feet and started nervously pacing.

He said he would be back by now, and he wasn't. What should I do?

The smart thing would be to wait it out, but what if he was hurt or found, or captured, or …dead? I shook my head. I couldn't; I wouldn't, think like that.

I would give him a few more hours. He did have to be careful with this movements. He probably needed to lay low for a bit until it was safe. But what about me? Was I just supposed to wait here, like a sitting duck?

I scoured the house looking for something I could defend myself with, but I came up short. This man had no weapons.

I smacked my forehead with my hand when I remembered why Nasol was so comfortable leaving me here alone – we were in the house of the castle chef. I made my way back to the kitchen and pulled open all the drawers. Of course, the last drawer held what I was looking for. Lucky for me, I had options. I grabbed two of the smaller knives and three of the big knives and laid them on the counter.

What I was going to do with five knives, I didn't know – I hadn't completely thought this plan through. But the more I had, the better I felt about being alone.

I walked back to the living room and sat down on the couch and waited.

And waited…

And waited…

One hour turned to three. Which quickly turned to six. Which then turned into eight. At the beginning of the ninth hour and the overall fourteenth hour of Nasol's absence, I was ready to lose my mind. I started to pace around the living room again waiting for Nasol to come back, debating if I should go after him. I didn't know the planet at all, but there had to be a way. I heard a light rustle from the back door and grabbed one of the knives and stood ready to strike if need be. Finally, the door opened, and Nasol walked through looking extremely tired.

"You're back!" I dropped the knife and rushed to him, throwing my arms around him pulling him into a tight hug.

"You're safe." He breathed in my ear as he wrapped his arms around me. We stayed like that for a moment before I finally broke our hug; Nasol pulled back slowly. After so much change in such a short time, I couldn't bear to lose him as well.

"Did you get what you needed?" I asked breaking the tension.

He nodded shutting the door behind him. I noticed he had a bag draped over his shoulder. A bag he didn't leave with, I noted. He slowly lowered it to the ground. "I got in contact with Vikram. He will not be able to get back here until tonight. Until then we can stay here. Has anyone been around yet?"

I shook my head.

"That means they have not made it to this side of town yet. But they will. I saw that they started doing checks in what remains of the city."

"Is that why you were gone for so long?" I asked finally taking a seat in one of the chairs.

He nodded. "They have waves of their people from the south coming up. Some of the police and people have tried to fight back, but they were quickly overrun and killed." He cursed under his breath, or I think it was a curse, I'm not sure what is a curse word on this planet. "My people are dying, and I am powerless to stop it."

"This is not your fault," I said. "I don't know much about this, but you can't take this weight all by yourself. This attack came out of nowhere. You thought you were finally at peace…there was no way to expect this and no reason for you to have a plan in response to an attack like this."

He didn't answer, but he seemed to agree with me, or at least I hoped he did. He could not blame himself; this was not his fault. We would make this right. We *would* get revenge for the murder of our parents.

"What else did you get?" I asked motioning to the bag at our feet.

"I got us some new clothes. You cannot wear that every day." He motioned to my dinner attire from two nights before. Had it really only been less than forty-eight hours? I pushed the thought away as I didn't want to break down again, especially not in front of Nasol. "Oh," he continued, "I got us some food." He pulled out the clothes and a few items of what I guess was food.

It looked like what I first ate on the ship with Vikram and smelled like it as well. I took a big bite of it; I was starving. He reached back into the bag and pulled out some guns.

"Why do you have those?" I asked swallowing another bite of the white flaky food brick as I reached for a second. I guess all the worrying kept my hunger at bay, but that was done now. Now, all I wanted to do was eat.

"We need to defend ourselves," he said as he handled the gun. "I ran into a few guards on my way back. Thankfully, I was able to take them by surprise and get these. If we run into any more trouble, we will need these."

"I don't know how to use those." I backed away, but he reached out and grabbed my hand and pulled me back.

"You cannot run from this," he said as he handed the gun over to me. "Keep this on you at all times. If you ever need to use it, just point and pull the trigger." He ordered, and I nodded. He picked up the clothes he mentioned and held them out to me.

I took the strips and held them up to my body. "I know the material here is special and all, but do you really think this will fit me?"

"It's not like I had a chance to look, but it stretches. It will fit."

I looked at him and back at the scraps in my hand. They looked like they were made for a doll, and not a life size one. There was no way they were going to fit, but I had been in my dinner dress for nearly forty-eight hours and, honestly, I was desperate for a change. I picked up a third flaky white brick finished it in three bites.

"What!" I rolled my eyes at Nasol's stare. "I'm hungry."

"I did not say anything." Nasol raised his hands in mock surrender.

"I'm going to go shower."

"Do you know how to use it?" He asked as I started towards the stairs.

"I'm sure I can figure it out." I sniped and walked to the bathroom. But of course, just like almost everything else, the showers on this planet were different. The general idea was the same, but the execution was different.

"Shower, ten-minutes, medium heat," I said, the water poured out of the shower head as I peeled myself out of my ruined dress. I slowly stepped into the shower and stood under the water. I stood there, in the silence and darkness, eyes closed, as I let the water wash over me, cleansing my body. I just wanted the water to erase the terrible situation that I was forced into.

Ten minutes later, the water shut off and I continued to stand there in the darkness and silence.

What was I supposed to do? What could I do? I couldn't help in this situation, but I couldn't leave either. I felt as though I was now a part of this; they made sure of that when they...

I forced myself to stop. I wouldn't; I couldn't think like that. Nasol wasn't falling apart and neither could I. He had lost more than I did in this situation if and he was staying together, so could I.

"Are you done yet?" I heard Nasol yell through the door.

"One second," I yelled back. "Dry please," I instructed. The shower changed, and warm air surrounded me, drying me off quickly. Once dry, I hopped out of the shower and pulled the scraps of fabric on. It turned out to be leggings and a tight black top. I gave myself a quick once over in the mirror, it was form fitting, but it would have to do – it wasn't like I had any other options.

I opened the door to see Nasol leaning against the wall. He gave me a quick once-over. "See it fits," he nodded.

I did a mock twirl for him. "It's a bit tight, but I guess I can live with it." I walked past him and down the hall. I waited for a few seconds and heard the water running once more.

I went back downstairs and walked over to his bag. There was more food sitting next to his pack. I took out another portion of food and broke it in half and took a bite. My body wanted more, but I couldn't risk it. I didn't know when we would have access to an abundance of food or if we would have to share with Vikram once he came for us so we needed to preserve what we had for as long as we could. I thought about how much I already had already eaten and instantaneously felt remorse – that could've lasted us a couple of days.

Nasol came down the steps a few minutes later looking fresh and clean, dressed in black as well. "Vikram will be here in a few hours. You should get some sleep."

"Don't you need sleep as well? You look tired."

He shook his head. "I am fine."

"How are you still running?" I asked.

"We are built differently. My body requires sleeps less frequently than yours."

"How much sleep do you need?"

He shrugged. "About four, five hours a day."

"How much have you had in the last few days?"

"About three hours," he shrugged slightly. "But do not worry, I feel fine."

"Are you sure?"

"I am fine. I promise," he replied with a faint smile.

I nodded, accepting that I couldn't make him go to sleep no matter how hard I tried. I walked over to the couch and laid down while Nasol took a bite of food and sat in the chair opposite me. I didn't realize how tired I was until I closed my eyes. Before I knew it, I was sleep, and all too soon I was gently awoken by the sound of Nasol's voice.

"Come on we need to go." Nasol stood above me. I sat up and looked around. Nasol was standing in front of me with his bag over his shoulder and two guns in his hands.

I stood up, and he handed one of the guns over to me.

"Good?" He asked as I took the gun. I nodded and started towards the door. "Let's go."

Chapter Fifteen

I stood behind Nasol as he opened the back door which led directly to the woods. We had to go about a mile out to meet Vikram.

Nasol held my hand the entire way. He said it was to make sure we didn't get separated if we were ambushed, but part of me wondered if maybe it was for other reasons.

"How much longer?" I whispered after we walked for twenty minutes.

"Stop talking," he whispered back. I nodded and kept walking behind him. We walked/jogged for another ten minutes through the dark woods before he finally came to a stop. We were right outside of a clearing, hidden by the trees. I opened my mouth to speak again, but Nasol motioned for me to stay quiet.

We waited for another ten long silent minutes before I felt the wind start to whip around us. I looked up and saw an aircraft the size of the four RVs heading towards us.

"Shit, he was seen." Nasol cursed. Flying behind the aircraft were three smaller ships all firing at Vikram's ship.

"What do we do?" I asked.

Nasol didn't answer. Instead, he dropped my hand and lifted his gun. He adjusted something on the dial and started firing. He missed the first of the smaller aircraft but hit the second and third causing a small explosion. The ships flew out of the sky and landed with another blast.

Vikram flew back around and landed in front of us. A door opened. "Run!" Nasol ordered firing up into the sky. I ran to the door as fast as I could as shots rang out around me. Nasol continued firing up at the other ship as he ran behind me. I climbed on board the vessel, and the door closed right as Nasol climbed on after me.

Nasol grabbed my hand and pulled me through the maze of hallways as the ship took off. We collided against the walls as the vessel took sharp turns to evade the people following us.

He only let go of my hand once we reached the cockpit, though I wasn't not sure what they were called on these ships. What a thing to think about while people were trying to kill us. He opened the door just as Vikram made a sharp turn almost flipping the vessel.

"Just go up!" Nasol yelled. "They can't follow you into space; their ships are too small." Vikram nodded gritting his teeth as he yanked the controller back. I fell back screaming as my back collided with the wall behind me.

"I don't like this!" I screamed as I felt the force glue me to the wall.

Finally, after what seemed like forever, we leveled out, and I collapsed to my feet. "Never, and I mean never, do that again." I gasped as I struggled to catch my breath.

Vikram pushed some buttons, moved some levers, and got up out of his seat. "I am glad you are alive," he said as he helped me to my feet.

Nasol was standing near the front of the ship, typing something on to a screen.

"Thank you. Me too," I said wiping my hands off on my pants before giving him a tight hug. Vikram seemed to hesitate before he returned the hug.

"What are we doing now?" I asked once I finally pulled away.

"We are going to go to one of our allies," Nasol said. "They will help us in this time of war. I know that Borran would have tried to keep this quiet until he had the planet under control, it is my guess we will be able to get there before he realizes who got on the ship."

"Ok," I said as I sunk into the chair behind Vikram.

"We will be there in a few days," Nasol said, "but I have sent a message ahead to the royal family with the instructions my parents left for times like this. They will be ready for us."

"And we can trust them, right?" I asked.

"Yes," Nasol said. "The King is my grandfather; my mother was his only daughter. He had four sons until he had her. She was his youngest and his favorite. We can trust him."

"Oh," I whispered. "Well since we're on the ship you should get some rest," I said. "You haven't slept in days."

"I am fine." He said but didn't believe him.

"You are not," I said as I folded my arms across my chest. "You haven't slept since the attack. You need rest."

Vikram shot Nasol a look and said something in their language, Nasol hissed something back, but Vikram held his ground. Nasol sighed and left the cockpit.

"What did you say to him?" I asked once we were alone.

"I just reminded him that you are correct, that he needs rest."

"Oh. Thanks," I smiled moving to take a seat next to him.

"I'm am sorry about your father," Vikram said after a minute of silence. "It is most unfortunate that he died as well. Your homecoming was supposed to be a joyous occasion."

"Yeah. Well…," I said and stared out the window.

"What are you thinking about?" He asked after a moment.

I shook my head. "Everything…and nothing at the same time." I let out a deep sigh as I finally started to feel the weight of my present reality. I could feel the tears begins to well in my eyes, "It's just…a lot to take in." With all the running, and waiting, and hiding, I hadn't taken a moment to really feel, well, anything except for anxiety and fear.

"Abriana, it's okay." Vikram reached out and grabbed my hand giving it a little squeeze.

"It's not okay." I sobbed as the dam broke again and I was unable to control myself. "He's dead, and he's never coming back!" I swallowed trying to control myself, but I was failing.

"I know," he whispered.

"I know this is stupid," I whispered into my hands. "I know I'm not the only one here that lost someone," I sniffed, "and in the grand scheme of this horrible situation I probably lost the least."

"Do not say that." Vikram stood and pulled me into his arms hugging me in a way that was very much needed. "He was your father, the only parent you ever had until very recently. You have had to face a lot of changes in the last couple of weeks only for it to end in his death. It is expected that you would feel this way."

"Nasol hasn't broken down," I said leaning into his arms. It felt familiar.

I felt him sigh and drop his head on mine. "This is going to sound morbid Abriana but, as much as this hurt, we are used to this. When I was young, at the height of the war, I prepared for the death of my parents." I gasped but didn't speak. "I have known since a young age that their death could come at the hands of our enemies. Their death hurts, but I grieved it a long time ago. You were thrown into this mess with no warning of the dangers it entailed. It is not good to bottle up your emotions."

"I..., wanted to get to know her," I whispered feeling fresh tears well up as I admitted my truth. "For years, I prayed my mother would come back. That the rumors I overhear my father's family saying about her weren't true. Every birthday all I wanted was for her to come back so I could understand why. To finally meet someone in my family that I looked like. Do you know what it is like to walk down the street with your father and people give you strange looks because you look nothing like him? To have family photos where you always stand out? I always wanted to know where I came from and I finally had that chance, and now, it's gone. I'll never get to know her, to understand her." I wiped my eyes.

"You are more like her than you know," Vikram said after a moment.

I smiled and grabbed his hand and gave it a squeeze. "Thank you," I whispered.

"You're welcome," he whispered and gave my hand a squeeze back then let go.

"So, the planet we are going to, tell me about it," I said changing the subject.

"It is called Enia."

"Can't we use warp speed or something to get there?" I joked.

"Your Earth movies are inaccurate," Vikram laughed. "There is no such thing as warp speed."

"Oh." I felt my face flush with embarrassment, but a thought occurred to me. "How do you know about movies from Earth?"

"Not only humans live there," Vikram said. "Many aliens can pass as human, they send..." He trailed off as he seemed to think of the right words, "They send care packages out, copies of movies, clothes, and other items they think their families will like."

"Why not tell Earth that there are other planets out there? Why don't you show yourselves? I mean you thought Earth would be the next planet."

"Do you believe that is a good thing? From what we are told, Earthlings are not the most understanding when it comes to differences if we show ourselves to them before they are ready."

"Yeah I understand that, but," I smiled, "I promise you most people on Earth would kill to meet you, or any alien, for that matter. Most would love to get off the planet."

"It is not just one planet's decision to make. We believe the planet must discover other life themselves."

"Why?"

"So, they can meet the other planets and people on their terms. If we were to land on Earth, announce that aliens are real and that we have been around for thousands of years, living amongst them, watching them, what do you think would happen?"

I nodded understanding him, most countries on Earth did have a shoot first, ask questions later type of mentality.

"Let's say Earth finally develops the right kind of technology to discover life outside of its solar system. Then what?" I asked.

"The last time this happened I was a child. Nasol would be better to speak to regarding this matter."

"Nasol is finally sleeping I won't wake him for this. Please just tell me." I asked wanting to keep the conversation going on something other than my pain.

"A group of ambassadors are sent to the planet to meet with the highest up of each nation, something like your United Nations. It can sometimes take anywhere from a couple of months to a year to gain their trust. They also only do this in times of peace to make sure we do not bring anyone into war. In the case of the Earth, we would have sent the most humanoid aliens. Our presentation would be broadcast worldwide to keep the chance of misinformation at bay. During the presentation, we would show our worlds and some of our technology."

"Has it ever gone wrong, to your knowledge?"

Vikram nodded. "It has gone terribly wrong in some cases. We have lost some ambassadors to other worlds where fear and hate have thrived. Thankfully those worlds were not capable of interstellar flight."

"Now that I really think about it, I think Earth would be a toss-up on the readiness scale." I laughed.

Chapter Sixteen

"Wow," I breathed as the new world came into view. It was huge, at least twice the size of Earth. "This is where your mother is from?" I asked Nasol.

He nodded. "Yes, it is very different from my world."

"It's big."

He nodded again taking the ship closer. We flew down until I could start to make out the outlines of the city.

"Where are we landing?" I asked.

"The high palace is at the top of the planet," Nasol explained steering the ship higher.

We flew for another twenty minutes in silence, and although I had plenty of questions, Nasol was giving off the air not wanting to talk. It was annoying, but I understood. He was focused on what would happen once we landed.

The palace came into view shortly. "Wow," I exhaled, staring up at the castle. I thought Nasol's castle was large, but it had nothing on this one. "It's beautiful."

"It is nice." He said, and I could see right though it– nothing is good enough for him. We flew down to the runway and landed with a small bump. Nasol opened the cargo door and nearly ran off the ship. Vikram and I slowly followed behind him.

We were greeted by two men, Nasol's grandfather, King Xan Arlox and Nasol's uncle, Prince Asher.

"Nasol!" King Xan pulled him into a tight hug. "Thank the stars you are alive. Your grandmother is worried sick about this entire situation."

'I guess introductions are going to be ignored,' I thought as I stood off to the side quietly.

"We need to act at once grandfather," Nasol said pulling back. "They are slaughtering my people in the street."

"We will talk about this once we are inside." Prince Asher said, ushering us inside a car that sped away as soon as the door shut.

"We don't have time for that." Nasol urged. "We need to act now! I sent my message days ago. That should have been enough time to establish a plan of attack."

"It is not that simple." King Xan replied, "You know the rules Nasol."

"Rules, what rules?" I asked. The men in the car all turned to look at me for the first time since our arrival, but it was Nasol's uncle, Prince Asher, who answered me.

"Part of the Inter-Worldwide Agreement is, outside planets do not get involved in internal planetary issues."

"Excuse me?" I asked not sure I was understanding. "You mean you won't help?"

"It means we *cannot* help." King Xan corrected. "Many years ago, when we first formed the interplanetary alliances, it was for an outward issue first and foremost. Part of that agreement was outside planets cannot help if a planet is having internal issues."

"This isn't just an internal issue," I interrupted. "It's a coup! He killed my parents. He killed your daughter. You have to help."

King Xan closed his eyes, and I felt Nasol glare at me. "It is not for you to speak about things you do not fully understand."

"I understand enough. I understand that we need your help – that your grandson needs your help."

"I have spoken to the council about this attack and they will let us know of their decision in a day's time."

"Who knows how many more people will die in a day's time," I said. "How many more families will be ripped apart."

King Xan trained his hard eyes on me, but I didn't lower my gaze. We were on his planet for less than ten minutes, but I already knew he wasn't going to help us. "The council will let me know of their decision. Until then, we will not discuss this any further."

I opened my mouth to speak again, but Vikram shook his head, so I held my tongue. I knew Nasol would do everything in his power to get justice for his planet and my parents and taking my anger out on his grandfather wasn't going to help our current situation. I realized that I really needed to think before I speak; I couldn't make an enemy out of our only ally. I swallowed and looked out the window at the passing scenery. It didn't feel like we were going fast but then the world outside the window was a blur of lines.

Not soon enough we arrived at the castle. If I thought Nasol's castle was massive, I was mistaken. This castle dwarfed his.

I must have been caught staring because once we exited the car, Vikram whispered. "The entire royal family lives here. Including the king and his family, his siblings and their families. It has been that way for generations."

I nodded my head and continued to be mesmerized by the massive structure.

We were ushered inside the castle as quickly as possible, but while Nasol was taken with his grandfather and uncle, Vikram and I were shown to what can only be described as a royal waiting room.

"Why are we being separated?" I asked Vikram once we were alone.

"It is a procedure. They will speak amongst themselves and will let us know of their decision."

"And why can't we be part of the meeting? My family was killed as well."

"Abriana-" Vikram started, but I cut him off.

"No, I should be in there. I want that bastard who killed my parents to pay. And if the conversation in the car says anything, they want be doing anything about it. That's bull."

"It is the way."

"Well, *the way* is stupid. Why would that rule even exist?"

Vikram guided me to a seat and sat across from me. "When the interplanetary system was first created, that rule was not in place. When planets had struggles within themselves, the rest of the planets in the system would take sides. Which ultimately led to conflicts between the other planets as well. There was a time when all the planets were involved in some way, shape, or form in one planet's internal struggles. So, the rule was made to stop that from happening. If a planet has its own internal conflict, the planet is placed under quarantine until it is stabilized again."

"Is that what happened when I was born?"

Vikram nodded. "Our planet was cut off for almost ten years. It's a hard law, but it works. It allowed us to work out our differences without the input or influence of other planets."

"What about if one planet attacks another?"

Vikram sighed. "That has happened, and it becomes a case by case decision. Most of the time the council will decide based on why the war was brought on in the first place."

"In cases like this, how do you think they are going to rule? This isn't a conflict; it's murder. They blew up the castle. It's not like the only people they killed were from Elendil. Ambassadors from other planets were there, at the Gala, I met them. This isn't a simple conflict. Can't they intervene on that basis alone?"

"The decision is the councils to make. I am sure that they were made aware of the circumstances of the attack. If King Xan goes against the wishes of the council, Enia could be pushed out of the interplanetary system. That could mean millions of his people would be out of a job. There will be no protection if they are attacked by a planet outside of the planetary system. Although there were other individuals from other planets present, the underlying issue is an internal one, and that's what they will base their decision on. Ambassadors understand the risk involved in living on another planet. Death is an assumed risk. If he acts without the support of the council, his people will suffer."

"So, the council will sit by and allow the murderer of his child, a princess of this land, and of innocent people to rule over a land that was taken by force?"

Vikram lowered his eyes refusing to meet mine. "This would not be the first time."

Chapter Seventeen

We waited for another twenty long minutes before Nasol graced us with his presence.

"How did it go?" I shot up from my seat, too nervous to wait. "What did they say?"

"They need more time," he said.

"More time for what? What do they need to think about?"

"You," Nasol said.

"Me? I don't understand. What do I have to do with their decision?" I asked, extremely confused.

"They intentionally killed your father, knowing he wasn't from our planet. With our rules, they know that is an act of war."

I shook my head. "All of these rules, they don't make any sense, but I am not one to kick a gift horse in the mouth. But is it enough for them to allow us to retaliate? I'm fine but wait," I looked back at him as he took a seat across from Vikram, "the death of your parents isn't enough to get the council to take action?"

He sighed. "My first-hand account of what happened was enough to move them a bit, but the death of an individual who is outside of our interplanetary alliance, especially a place like Earth, could lead to war and discord."

I snorted. "That's bull. I love my dad, but he was a nobody in your world. Why would his death..." I trailed off as the realization hit me and Nasol had a ghost of a smile on his lips. "They're using him to create a loophole."

Nasol nodded. "I hope you don't mind."

"No," I shook my head. "I'm fine with any reason they use as long as it gets them to act. When do we leave?"

"You will not be joining us," Nasol said.

"Excuse me?" I was a bit taken back, "What do you mean? Of course, I am helping. They killed the only parent I'd ever known."

"It would be unwise for you to take part in the fight," Vikram interjected. "You have not been trained to fight, or shoot a gun, or fly a fighter jet. You would be more of a liability than an asset."

"I can learn," I said crossing my arms over my chest.

"You will not take part," Nasol repeated.

"You're fighting," I retorted.

He nodded. "Abriana, I will get him for killing our families, but I cannot do that and protect you as well."

"You don't have to protect me!" I was not a child. I didn't need to be protected from everything. Given what I had gone through, I deserved the right to fight! Although I knew he was capable, I felt as though I should be the one to avenge the death of my parents, not Nasol.

"You know nothing of my world Abriana. You know nothing of how war works – how it is fought and won. I have to go back to Elendil to lead them in the fight. People will die. This could go on for years."

I turned to Vikram. "Do you agree with him?"

Vikram nodded.

"And what do you expect me to do while you two are off fighting?" I asked pushing back tears of frustration.

"I expect you to stay here, and stay safe," Nasol said matter-of-factly.

"When will you leave?" I asked.

"Once the council approves the action, I will make an attack plan with my uncles."

"What's the timeline for this?" I asked, trying to weasel out as much information as I could.

"I hope just a day."

"So soon? So, you're just going to leave me on a random planet and go off to fight a war? A war, might I add, that both of you might not survive. What am I supposed to do then?"

"Abriana," Nasol reached for me.

"No! Don't touch me!" I screamed. "I can help, I can be useful! Vikram said I was like my mother well let me prove it! Let me be useful. I want- no I need to help!".

"Abriana!" Nasol caught ahold of my arm before I could reach the door. He spun me around to face him. "This is not the time to act like this."

"Then tell me how I am supposed to act then. Everything in my life has been ripped away from me in the most violent ways possible! I know what my body smells like on fire, because of your planet's problems! I was ripped away from the only home I've ever known. My father is dead, the mother I always wanted is dead, and I am being left behind on a planet I've never heard of while the only two people I know in this galaxy go off to fight in a war where they may very well die! Please, *please* tell me how I am supposed to process this?"

"I don't have an answer!" Nasol screamed. I could see the fire in his eyes and a crack in his steely facade. "I know you are not happy with my decision, but it is my decision! I will not apologize for trying to do what is best to keep you safe! How are you not getting that? I have more than just your well-being to worry about. I have millions of people who are scared and frightened about what is going on. I have to think about them as well. I have to let them know I am still fighting for them. You are not trained for this, for any of it, and in war, bringing you will only hinder us." He stared at me for a second before leaving the room.

Chapter Eighteen

"Hi!" A peppy voice woke me from my sleep. I pushed the covers back and pushed myself up on the bed. A blue girl stood at the foot of my bed with a tray of food in hand.

"Umm..." I rubbed my eyes. "Hello?" I slowly sat up as memories from yesterday replayed over in my mind.

"Hi, I'm Daneer." She walked around the bed and placed the tray of food across my lap. And yes, I'm blue." She answered as if seeing the question form in my head. "It's the first question most humans have once they meet a light mage for the first time." She smiled.

"Light mages?" I thought for a moment. "Like the ones that were on Nasol's Planet?" I picked up the fork and starting poking at the food and took a small bite. Surprisingly it was pretty good.

She nodded. "They are a distant relation. Though my people are not as powerful as them."

"What do you mean?" I asked.

"There are multiple species of light mages, those who were on Nasol's planets were from another planet."

"Oh ok." I nodded thinking I understood and moved to another thought. "You've met other humans?" I continued to take small bites of the food on my plate.

"Yes," she smiled. "Very few know about the world outside of Earth, but I have met my fair share of those who have decided to live life off Earth."

"And there are more like you, who are blue?" I asked and instantly shut my eyes at the stupidity of my question.

If she was offended, she didn't let it show, she just smiled at me. "It's ok. I'm from Cerulean."

"The color?"

"I guess you could say that," she nodded. "Everyone on my planet is a shade of blue. We range from what you would call midnight all the way to sky blue."

"Oh," I nodded, following along. "That's cool. It's the same thing for black people on Earth." I said rubbing my arms.

"I like my blue skin of my people, no matter the shade." She hugged herself, and I felt a kinship with her for that statement.

"Well, it does suit you."

She smiled at me, "I like you! I know we are going to be great friends."

"Just like that?" I laughed taking a few more bites. It was pretty good, it reminded me a bit of bacon and eggs.

"Yes. I am your personal servant while you are staying here, so I do hope we get along."

I picked up the cup and took a sip of the juice. It was a bright yellow like orange juice but had the distinct flavor of coffee. "Yellow coffee?" I almost gagged.

"Do you not like it?" Her face fell.

"No! No, no," I rushed out trying to save the conversation. "It's just I'm not used to it. That's all."

"Oh, okay." Her face brightened up again. "That' good then! I'm glad you like it. I worked hard on your meal."

"Will you be cooking all of my meals?"

Daneer nodded enthusiastically. "Breakfast and lunch, and I will be here to assist you with anything you require while on this planet. The King asked for me."

"Wow." I took another sip of the coffee-like drink. "Then I guess he must think highly of you, or..." I trailed off. I didn't think I made a good impression with the King; she might not be the best.

"I am very honored!" Daneer smiled. "I did not know the King knew who I was. It is a great honor to serve you."

"I'm not so sure," I muttered.

"What would you like to do today?" Daneer asked.

I looked at her and pondered my answer. "Before I do anything, I would like to talk to Vikram and Nasol."

"Oh." Daneer looked down. "You don't know?"

"What?"

"They left."

"What do you mean?"

"They left early this morning. They needed to take the first ship off the planet. The council asked for them to attend the meeting personally, so they could discuss the next course of action. It takes a few days to get there. The council wants to convene in four days' time."

"They just left without saying bye," I whispered feeling my stomach turn over and suddenly I was no longer hungry.

"I believe they wanted to get there as soon as possible."

"Oh." I leaned back in bed and pulled the cover over me once more.

"Are you ok?" Daneer asked.

"Um, I'm just tired." I lied. "It's been a few hectic days. Do you think I could go back to sleep?"

Daneer nodded. "I will be just outside the room if you need anything."

I waited until I heard the door close before I let the first tear fall...and the anger sweep through me!

Those- those jerks, those assholes! They left me!

They didn't have the balls to say goodbye to me. To look me in the eyes before they left me behind.

Chapter Nineteen

I laid in bed for hours before I finally decided to pull myself together. It hurt that the only people I knew in the system left without a word, but I couldn't wallow in bed all day until they returned. I got up and threw on some clothes I found in the closet.

"Daneer?" I called as I walked to the door to my room.

"Hi!" Daneer smiled as I opened the door. "Are you ready to explore the castle?"

"I was hoping we could go to the gym? I would like to get a workout in."

"Perfect!" She smiled. "Right this way." She started walking down the hall, and I followed her. This castle was twice the size of Nasol's, so it took a bit longer to get to the gym.

Once we arrived, I was amazed, although I shouldn't have been. Their gym, like the rest of the house, was twice as large as Nasol's gym.

"What would you like to do?" Daneer asked.

"Do you have a punching bag?" I asked, looking around.

"Why do you need a punching bag?" A voice came from behind me.

"You're highness." Daneer bowed. I followed her example and bowed as well. "Prince Jabo, this is Abriana from Earth and Elendil. Abriana this is Prince Jabo, Nasol's cousin."

"Hello Prince Jabo," I bowed again.

"Just call me Jabo, I'm only a prince in name; I have no claim to the throne." Jabo winked. I finally looked up to take him in. He was taller than Nasol and a bit stockier than Vikram. He had short cropped black hair that had a small curl to it, and he had playful mauve eyes. "My father is the second son of the King, so I will never rule. Not that I want to. I truly enjoy having all the perks and none of the responsibility."

"You don't sound too put out because of that," I laughed.

"That's because I'm not. There would be too much pressure if I was next in line. Nope," he shook his head, "my job is to look pretty and attend royal functions."

"That can't be your only job," I laughed as I started walking around the small gym, trying to get a feel of the room.

He shrugged as he followed behind me. "No, I'm in the military as well. Most men in my family go into the military. What better way to serve our people than to serve our people?" He laughed at his joke.

"Oh, well I'm sorry if I interrupted your workout. I just wanted to get one in myself." I said.

"You're fine. It's not every day a cute Earthling is staying in the castle." He winked; and I bit back a laugh. "Oh, feisty. I like it."

"Whatever," I laughed. I could tell when someone was just a flirt by nature.

"I believe you asked about a punching bag? There's one in that corner over there." He pointed behind him. "Do you need a spotter?"

"Oh," I waved him off. "I don't want to take up any more of your time. I'll be fine."

"No, I insist." He said. "You are a guest in our kingdom. It would be my honor."

"I will wait outside." Daneer bowed and walked out the door.

Jabo watched her go and then led me to the back of the room where a few punching bags hung. He walked over to a small closet and pulled out some gloves and tossed them over to me. I scrambled to put them on while he stood behind the bag.

"Let's see what the Earthling can do," he winked as he held the bag.

I finished strapping on the gloves and turned to face him.

"Give me your best shot," he taunted. I narrowed my eyes and got into my boxing stance. I'd never actually worked with a punching bag before, but there was a first time for everything. I had so much aggression to get out of my system, and that seemed like the safest method. I took a breath and threw a punch.

"Come on," Jabo taunted. "You can do better than that. Give it another go."

I rolled my shoulder and tried again.

"See, it is better now," he encouraged. "Again."

I took a deep breath and recalled my training with Vikram before the attack. Though it was only a few short days, he did teach me a couple of combos. I rolled my shoulder, readjusted my stance and started the combos. Jab, jab, cross. Jab, jab, cross. Jab, jab, cross, left hook, cross. Jab, cross, left hook, cross.

"Toss in a kick," Jabo called out, and I did. I brought my left knee up and rammed it into the bag.

"Good." Jabo praised from his spot behind the bag. "I see someone has some aggression to get out this morning."

"I. Don't. Know. What. You. Are. Talking. About." I punctuated each word with a punch or kick to the bag.

"So, this doesn't have anything to do with my cousin leaving so early this morning?"

I repeated my prior denial, this time hitting the bag with a little bit more fervor than before. I might have verbally denied the connection, but my hits might have confirmed it.

Jabo chuckled as he recoiled from one of my hits. "Sure, but if it makes you feel any better, he asked me to look out for you."

That caught my attention.

I stopped throwing punches and looked at Jabo, the confusion I felt was probably clearly displayed on my face. "Wait, what? Why?"

Jabo shrugged. "He just came by early this morning and asked me to look after you while they were off planet."

"Why you?" I asked resuming my hits.

He shrugged again. "Probably because I'm his favorite cousin and he won't have to worry about any competition from me."

"What?" I dropped my arms. "Competition for what?"

Jabo stared at me for a minute before a laugh erupted from his lips. "You don't know? Oh, this is rich." He howled with laughter.

"What don't I know?" I huffed.

"You're his mate!" Jabo laughed.

"What? No, I'm not!"

"Then why did he tell me you were?" I didn't know Jabo well enough to know whether he was lying or not. But the feeling I had in the pit of my stomach, gave me the inclination that he was telling the truth about Nasol's request and confession. But I was confused – wasn't mating supposed to be a mutual thing? He had to be messing with me. Nasol had been nothing but rude and mean to me until the night of the explosion. This had to be a lie. But since the explosion he had been different, but again that didn't mean I was his mate. It meant that he was more focused on our situation than being a jerk and not that he kept his promise to be different.

"I don't know?" I shook my head. "But you're wrong; I'm not his mate."

"Oh yes, you are." He smiled. "But denial is a normal response; my mate tried to deny it when I first met her."

"You're married?" I asked, getting back into fighting stance.

"Naw, not yet." He smiled. "She's still in denial. But I'm wearing her down."

"So, she doesn't love you?"

"No," Jabo shook his head. "And to be honest, I don't love her either. I don't know her well enough to, but mating doesn't equate to love. That would be like some kind of mind control."

"I'm not his mate," I said as I refocused my attention on the bag.

Jabo just chuckled. "Whatever you say."

I shook my head and refocused on my hits. Thankfully he didn't bring it back up, and we concentrated on my workout. After twenty more minutes on the bag, we switched to hand to hand combat, and I got my butt kicked. Unlike Vikram, Jabo believed the best way to learn was by failure. Though I will admit, I did learn a few new moves from him.

Only after I was a sweaty, sore mass, barely able to stand, did he finally call Daneer back into the room.

"Help her into the healing tub," Jabo ordered.

"Did you have to be so rough with her?" Daneer scolded rushing in. She quickly threw one of my arms over her shoulder and helped me to the bathroom.

"What?" Jabo held his hand up in defense. "We were sparring. I won."

"I had no chance," I argued back as Daneer practically dragged me to the bathroom. Once inside she pulled me to the back where the tubs were. She helped me out of my outer layer of clothing and helped me into the vat.

I sighed as the warm water rushed over my body.

"Feel better?" Daneer asked.

"So much better." I moaned.

"Good!" She smiled. "Did you have a good workout? Were you able to get out all of your aggression?"

"What do you mean?" I asked feigning ignorance.

Daneer smiled. "Your aggression," She repeated. You were upset that they left without saying goodbye. Were you able to work all of that out?"

"Oh, that. Yeah... I guess." I sighed leaning back and thought over Jabo's words. I couldn't be Nasol's mate. I closed my eyes and thought over our past interactions, and it was starting to add up. He told Vikram to train me, and that I needed to control my emotions more. I needed to worry about who I was representing. Hell, his mother even said I looked like a princess, and on the balcony, he wasn't kidding. He was my mate, and he left me.

Chapter Twenty

"Looks who's up," Jabo yelled across the courtyard Daneer was escorting me across. Jabo was surrounded by a couple of people who looked to be about his age. "Come over," he said as he hailed me over, "I'll introduce you."

I glanced at Daneer and realized there was no way for us not to go over and be not be viewed as rude. I nodded and walked over.

Jabo threw one of his hulking arms over my shoulder as soon as I was in arm's length.

"Guys, this is Abriana." He shook my shoulder slightly. "Abriana this is my sister Janessa, and these are my cousins Kameron and Pablo." They nodded at his introductions.

"The girl from Earth," Pablo said looking me up and down. "I've never seen one this close before."

"Oh, well yeah." I stumbled over my words not sure how I was supposed to answer.

"Don't mind him," Janessa said as she brushed him off. I looked at her with mild amazement and slight confusion. Had Jabo not introduced her as his sister, I would have never known they were related. While Jabo was tall and reminded me of a mini Hulk, Janessa was tiny and petite. They had differing eye color and hair color. Jabo had dark black hair Janessa had long soft brown hair, and her eyes were bright blue instead of mauve. "He's always 'putting his foot in his mouth' isn't that a common Earth saying?" She smiled.

"Yea, but how do you know it?" I asked.

"I spent a few months on Earth when I was a child. I had a distant aunt who lived there."

"Oh, I didn't know." I looked at Jabo. "Have you been to Earth?" I asked as I discreetly slid his arm from my shoulder.

"Naw," he laughed. "I had the option to go with her, but I didn't want to."

"He was scared." Janessa faked whispered, giving me a wink.

"I was not!" Jabo rebutted, earning a laugh from the others. "But where were you two off to?" Jabo motioned to Daneer.

"Oh!" I turned to her. "I'm sorry!" I had completely forgotten about her. "Daneer is showing me the grounds, letting me know where I'm allowed to go and where I'm not," I explained. "She's been amazing so far." I smiled at her.

"What have you seen so far?" Janessa asked.

"We were just getting started," I said. "But I've seen the gym and the library, and she was going to show me the pool."

"Do you like to swim?" Kameron asked eyeing me up and down.

"Cool it," Jabo said, his eyes narrowing on Kameron slightly.

"What?" He held his hand up in mock surrender. "I'm merely asking our guest if she likes to swim."

"She's spoken for," Jabo said.

Kameron rolled his eyes. "I do not believe she is tied to him yet. She can have fun if she so chooses."

Janessa hissed something at Kameron in another language, and he hissed something back before Jabo stepped in, raising his voice at Kameron.

Kameron hissed something, this time in my direction, before turning on his heels and leaving.

"What was that about?" I asked once everything calmed down.

"Just Kameron being stupid." Janessa sighed as she watched him walk away. "But in any event, don't let us distract you. Go enjoy your tour of the grounds."

"Sure." I agreed but I wasn't sure if I believed her explanation, but it didn't seem like this the time or place, I turned to Daneer, "Ready?"

"Yes," she smiled brightly and led the way.

"See you guys later," I called as I trailed after Daneer.

Once we were far enough away, I asked, "What were they really saying?"

"It's not my place to say," Daneer answered.

"Daneer, they were talking about me. I think I have a right to know what they were saying."

She sighed. "Prince Kameron knows who his mate is, but he despises her, so he makes a point to sleep with other women to hurt her more."

"Why doesn't he like her?" I asked.

"Prince Kameron cares for the outer appearance and social standing more than anything else. His mate does not meet the caliber he believes he should attract."

"What does she do?" I couldn't help myself; I had to know.

Daneer frowned slightly and hesitated before answering. "She is a maid, and a dear friend of mine."

"Oh," I said, suddenly realizing what happened. "He did that because you were there."

Daneer nodded. "He was making it known he did not respect the bond. But he is foolish."

"How so?"

"He-" She paused trying to find the right word. "He thinks she is lower than he is, but his actions have proven that he is the unworthy one. He has lowered himself in her eyes so much that his actions no longer hurt her."

I paused. "It's not you, is it?"

"No." Daneer smiled. "Thankfully it is not I, but she is from my planet. It's her skin color he despises most, and for that, she will never forgive him."

"I guess Jabo was right, being someone's mate doesn't make love."

"No," Daneer sighed. "Though it would help if some feelings came along with the mating. It would make the process so much smoother."

Chapter Twenty-One

I moved around my room debating what I wanted to do today. It had been three days since Nasol and Vikram left me on this planet and they had yet to reach out.

I wanted to say I wasn't hurt, but that was a lie. But Janessa, Daneer, and Jabo kept my days active enough to where I didn't miss them as much. However, this morning, Jabo was needed back on the base, Janessa had plans as well, and Daneer was covering for a servant who had fallen ill, thus, leaving me all alone.

I had already been to the gym and back; I was getting better every day, but I still had space to improve.

I sat and wondered if it was possible to talk to the King, to see what was going on with the council and if he had heard any word from Nasol.

I thought that maybe I should apologize for my behavior the last time we spoke as well.

I walked over to my closet and searched for a new outfit – I didn't think it would be respectful to go to him dressed in my gym clothes. I put on some of the more delicate items I had yet to try out. It took three wardrobe changes before I thought my outfit looked nice enough.

As I walked down the hall, I hoped I remembered the directions Daneer gave me. In her defense, though, she told me I wasn't allowed in the room.

It took a few tries, and a couple of twists and turns before I made it to the grand doors that Daneer told me led to where the King worked.

But maybe he wasn't in. Last time I was here, there were guards outside the room, and now there were none.

I thought about it for a bit. It shouldn't be a problem for me to knock, especially if no one was in there.

I walked to the door and raised my knuckle when I heard movement from inside the room. I pressed my ear up to the door trying to listen for more. I couldn't make out much, but it sounded like there was a scuffle happening inside the room. I pushed the door open and rushed in.

"What the-" I froze. The room was a mess. The desk was overturned, there were papers everywhere, broken furniture laid strewn around the room, and the King was standing with his back against the wall, his sword facing the two guards who had their swords trained on him in return.

One of the guards turned towards me, his sword outstretched. "You shouldn't have come in here." He growled at me, lunging for me. I jumped out of the way and grabbed the first thing I could reach to protect me. I lifted my hand and in it was a fire poker from next to the fireplace. I wasn't a sword fighter, but I wasn't going down without a fight.

"She has nothing to do with this," the King panted. He was holding his side as blood poured from it. "Leave her be."

"She's seen too much! She needs to die as well." The guard growled lunging back at the King. He dodged the attack and brought his sword down in a sweeping motion slicing through the guard like butter.

I couldn't stop the scream that escaped me as I saw the man fall. The guard facing me turned and rushed the King knocking the sword out of his hand and him on the floor. He raised his arms up ready to bring the sword down to finish the

King off, but somehow, crossed the room, and stabbed him in the neck with my poker. He gurgled as blood flowed down his chest. The sword fell from his hand and, thankfully, missed the King, and the guard fell to the ground.

"Are you ok?" I asked rushing to the King's side, helping him to his feet.

"I am fine." I helped him into one of the chairs that had yet to be broken.

"What happened?" I asked feeling sick as the thought that I killed a man filled my mind.

"The coup is spreading," he wheezed holding his side as more blood flowed from his wound. I couldn't think. Spreading? What should I do? I need to get him help; he was going to die. If the King died this would be bad, so very bad. I froze for a second trying to decide.

"I need to get you help," I said.

"No need," a new voice spoke up from the doorway. I turned and saw Prince Asher standing there with five guards standing behind him.

"Son," the King started. "The guards are staging a coup. They tried to take my life. We need to find those who are no longer loyal to the crown."

Prince Asher held up a hand, "Do not worry father. I know who is loyal," he paused. "to me."

I narrowed my eyes. "To you?" I asked in astonishment.

Prince Asher smirked and raised his arm; I felt my stomach drop as he held a gun and aimed it at his father. I screamed as he shot his father between the eyes.

Chapter Twenty-Two

"You bastard!" I screamed at Prince Asher lunging for him, but his guards grabbed me. "You can't do this." I struggled in his guard's grip, but it was useless, they were too strong. "Let me go!"

"Letting you go does nothing but hurt my plan," he laughed as he turned away from me. His men dragged me, kicking and screaming, behind him. With my father dead, I will be named King of Enia and I cannot have you out there with this knowledge."

"You can't just sweep this under the rug," I screamed, hoping that someone would hear me. The men dragged me down a back hallway I had never seen before.

"My father's death will be ruled a cost of war, and if anyone disagrees, I will make them rethink their position."

"So, you'd kill them too?" I spat at him. "How could you do this? How could you kill your own father? You're a monster!"

"You stupid little girl," he laughed. "My father was weak. He couldn't see the beauty of my plan."

"What plan?" I screamed again, hoping to attract some attention. "All you did was kill your father." They dragged me down some old rusty steps.

He snorted as he turned to me with cold eyes, "Who do you think help fund the attack on Elendil?"

I felt my stomach drop as he turned back around. "No," I whispered. "How could you do that to your own sister? You killed her! You killed my parents!" They threw me into a cell, but I quickly scrambled to my feet to face him.

"I have plans for this system, plans that they would not agree to. Plans they would try and stop. But they miscalculated."

"Miscalculated what?" I asked.

"Peace is not profitable. Peace makes you weak. We are spreading ourselves too thin caring about these new planets, bringing them in on the same level as us. No! We shall rule them! Show these inferior beings' real power. These people in power and their rules, I will put a stop to it all."

I felt bile rise in my throat at the sick thought. "You're going to go after the council?"

His smile revealed his answer. "Maybe you are not so stupid after all. I am going to show them that Elendil is just the beginning, I have big plans to reshape all of this into a new world order."

"And what about those who are fine with the way things are now?"

He shook his head. "Death will show them the light."

"And if you have to kill millions before they give in?"

"Then they will die like the trash that they are," he spat.

"They are not trash! They are strong, and they will fight you to the very end!"

"Their end has already come, my plan for the council meeting will see to that."

"How could you send Nasol to his death? He's your flesh and blood." I argued knowing that after the murder of his own father, his nephew wasn't that important on the family spectrum.

"Family who stands against you are just close enemies, and easier to kill." He said backing up from the cell. "Plus, Nasol was just the spawn of my whore sister. They stopped being family the moment she married off-planet."

"Then why am I still alive?" I asked. By Prince Asher's reasoning, I should've been dead, not a captive.

He paused looking me over. "You have connections that you still remain ignorant to. I may need a bargaining chip in the coming weeks. I should actually thank Nasol before I have him killed. I had no idea of your existence or that you were so close until he brought you here."

"I'm no one."

He smirked. "Oh, my child. How very little you really know."

Chapter Twenty-Three

I paced up and down my cell. I needed to wrap my head around the last few hours and try and figure out what my next steps where. The main problem that I needed to solve was how to warn Nasol if I still had time to.

I stopped pacing.

What if I was too late? What if he was already dead?

I shook the thought from my head. No, I couldn't think like that. He was smart, he was capable, and Vikram was with him. Between the two of them, they were smart enough and strong enough to face anything head on.

The next issue I pondered was: why was I still alive? Why didn't he kill me already? I wasn't a bargaining chip. Everyone I loved or had loved me was dead or, at least, thought that I was.

I sighed and dropped on my small cot. Who was I kidding? I was never going to get out of here alive. No one knew I was going to see the King and Prince Asher had probably swept the whole thing under the rug already. How did my life turn into this? I was just going for a run before I had me meet some friends to finish a school project. I was a normal teenager and now I'm sitting in a cell on an alien planet. My mom and dad were dead. Nasol and Vikram didn't know they were going to be betrayed. No one on this planet knew I was here. This is not how I wanted to die. This is not how it was supposed to end. I scrubbed my face with my palms and leaned back against the crumbling wall.

The wall!

I shot forward and turned around. The wall was *crumbling.*

I pressed my hand upon it. It was cold and damp like dirt.

I looked around and realized my cell was old, and for a castle as grand as this, there was no reason for a cell to be in this shape. Actually, there was no point to these cells. Why would they keep anyone here at the castle? These had to be old, out of date, and mostly dirt. I turned back to my cell bars. I couldn't see any guards out there, but that didn't mean they were not in earshot. I had to risk it. I glanced around the small dirt cell and realized there wasn't anything in here that I could use to dig. I glanced down at my clothes and shoes. The heel on my shoe was slightly broken in the shuffle with Prince Asher and his guards. I pulled my shoe off and broke off the heel.

I pulled my bed forward as quietly as I could, jumped behind it, and started digging. I had to make sure the hole stayed lower than the bed to ensure no one spotted it.

~

I dug for what seemed like hours and only made it about a foot in. I sighed, leaned back, and took a quick breather. I looked at the mess around me. I had a small pile of dirt at my feet.

I needed a way to effectively hide the dirt I was currently digging out. I picked up a small amount of dirt and moved it to the other corner and started to pat the dirt on the wall and took a step back.

It looked different but not noticeable. And to be honest, I didn't think anyone would stay down here long enough to realize what I was doing.

I took another deep breath and started digging again. I would scrape for ten seconds and pause to listen then scrape for another ten and pause and listen.

I did this for a few hours until my arms felt as though they were going to fall off. But I had made headway. I could fit the entire upper half of my body in the opening I was making. I wiped my arms along the dirty sheets and pushed the bed against the opening and dropped down on it. Before I knew it, I was sleeping.

~

I awoke again to the sound of footsteps and loud voices. I shot up and checked to make sure the hole was still covered. I sat and waited for the owners of the voices to appear.

It took a few minutes for them to arrive. I guess the sounds down here travel.

There were two guards walking towards me; the smaller one was holding a small tray.

"Hello, little Earthling." The taller guard sneered at me.

I didn't answer, just shrank back against the wall.

"Aww is the little Earthling scared?" The shorter guard laughed unlocking my cell door and dropping the tray of food on the floor. It hit the floor with a small thud spilling the contents over in the floor.

The guards laughed and turned to head back.

"Wait!" I called after them, they paused and turned back.

"Oh, now the little Earthling wants to talk." The taller one teased.

I swallowed. "Why am I here? Why am I still alive?"

The guards shared a laugh. "Are you saying you don't know?" The taller one laughed.

"Prince Asher said I have a connection that I remain ignorant of. I don't want to remain ignorant."

They laughed again, but the smaller one spoke up this time. "I don't see the harm in telling you since you will never see them anyway."

"Who?"

"Your mother's parents," he spat.

"I don't understand."

"Not our problem." The taller guard said. "Let's go, let's leave the little Earthling to her small cell."

They turned to leave and the smaller one called over his shoulder. "I wouldn't eat all of that today. We are not scheduled to bring you more food for another three days."

They laughed again and kept walking. This time, I didn't try to stop them when they left.

I waited until I couldn't hear them anymore before I crawled from my bed and over to the over-turned tray of food. It was ruined and covered in dirt. I didn't realize how hungry I was until the chance of food was falling just out of my grasp.

I wanted to cry... but I couldn't.

I wouldn't.

I had to be strong, and I had to find my way of this cell. I *would* find my way out of this cell. I swallowed and picked up the white block of food. I wiped as much dirt as I could and took a bite.

The urge to vomit hit me instantly but I pushed through and chewed the white block. It was close to the dino fish I had on Elendil but covered in gravelly dry dirt. The dirt coated my throat as I fought to swallow.

They brought me nothing to drink, so I forced myself to breathe through my nose until the urge to vomit subsided.

My stomach rumbled again, now aching for real food. I looked back down at the metal tray and decided against taking another bite.

I stood up to walk back to the hole when it hit me: the tray was metal. I quickly picked it up and tried to quiet my glee. I would be able to make way more progress using it to dig over the broken heel of my shoe.

I moved the bed out of the way and went back to digging, with a little bit more optimism.

~

I dug for two days..., or what I thought was two days. I wasn't sure. It was hard to keep track of the time down there. But I knew I needed to make some headway before the guards came back.

I knew by now Daneer, Jabo, and Janessa must've realized that I was missing and what their uncle did. He didn't seem like the type who would hide his work.

I sighed and backed my way out of the tunnel. I was exhausted, sore, and very hungry. On day two, I tried to eat more the of the food given to me, but I was unable to get any of it down better than my last try.

My tunnel was deep. I could fit three lengths of my body in there, but I was no closer to breaking out... or at least that's what I thought, and it was getting harder to hide in the dirt. I had to start stamping it in the ground as I could no longer get it to stay on the wall. If I didn't find the other side of the wall soon, I was going to run out places to hide the dirt.

My plan was to hold out until the next time they brought me food and escape after that. If they really were coming every three days that should give me enough time to get away. At least I hoped it would.

I leaned back on my small bed; I needed more rest before I could do anything else. I double checked that the hole was covered, and I closed my eyes.

Chapter Twenty-Four

When I woke, there was another tray with a few more scraps of dirty food in my cell and murky water for me to drink. They must have stopped by while I was sleeping. Dread filled my stomach at the thought. They could have seen the hole or noticed that what I was doing.

I rolled my body off the cot and picked up the molding white brick. I picked off a much mold as I could and took small bites of food forcing my body to keep it down.

I picked up my old tray and moved my bed and crawled back into the hole and started to dig once more. The further I dug into the wall the colder and more damp was the dirt. It was harder to dig, but I wouldn't give up.

'Up down, Up down, Up down' I repeated the mantra in my head over and over in my head to keep me focused on my task.

I pressed my hand down on the floor below me and felt a little give.

I scrambled back slightly and pressed my hand against the floor again. I felt it give a little more and I realized that I never thought about what was below me. I just assumed I was on the bottom level of the dungeon. But what if I wasn't?

I took the tray and scratched at the ground, scraping back and forth. I dug a few seconds more before a little hole appeared. I leaned down and peered through the hole, but I couldn't make out too much detail. But from what I could, there appeared to be a large room not too far below me.

I backed out of the tunnel and back to my cell. I needed to make a decision, the floor was too thin for me to dig over, it was either I go down into the dark room or stay in the cell.

"Damn it!" I screamed before controlling myself. "Calm down Abriana. You can do this. You are your mother's daughter; she was a strong woman. Everyone told you that you are so much like her. Make her proud."

I looked around. I knew I would never get out of this cell alive if I didn't get myself out.

I was going to get out of here.

I pulled the bed behind me to hide the hole and crawled back through the small opening I made. It was a lot darker now, but I clawed at the opening, and it slowly started to grow. I slowly backed up from the edges of the hole as it grew; I didn't want the floor to open under me. Once it was large enough for my body to fit through, I turned my body around and slid my legs through and dropped down.

Pain exploded up my left leg as I fell over and grabbed at my ankle. It felt like I shattered it. I swallowed hard and bit back my screams of pain. I looked up at the ceiling and realized I truly misjudged the size of the drop. I fell almost twenty feet. I was lucky I didn't hurt myself more.
I rolled over to my knees keeping my left ankle off the ground as much as I could.

I was in a hallway, a very old hallway, and the question I was now faced with was: which way should I go? I shuffled over to the wall and used it to pull myself up. Using the wall for support, I started to hobble the down the hallway on a downward slope. I took breaks every few minutes to give my ankle a quick break. After an hour of hobbling, my ankle throbbed with every breath. My chest burned, my arms were tired, and I was starting to get dizzy. I slid down the wall and closed my eyes and passed out.

I woke again to someone shaking me.

Chapter Twenty-Six

"Jabo?" I asked as his form came into focus. I could've sworn that he was leaning over me in the dark hallway, but he couldn't really be here, could he?

"Abriana? Shit. Are you ok?" He gently shook me again. "Here drink this." I felt him tip my head back and a lip of a bottle touch my lips, as cool water filled my mouth. I struggled to swallow and coughed a few times until he pulled the bottle away. "Hey, it's ok, slowly." He said slapping me on my back a few times.

I held my head waiting for the dizziness to pass.

"Are you really here or am I hallucinating?" I asked.

"It's me." He cupped my face making me focus on him.

"How?" I asked relief filling my voice.

"We've been looking for you for days," he said. "We've been crazy with worry. Asher said you were dead, that you ran into the guards who killed my grandfather but something about it seemed off. He wouldn't let us see the body, and there was no blood. Yesterday, Daneer told me she overheard some of Asher's guards laughing about the little Earthling they had locked up in the old cells and -" He trailed off. "But anyway, she came to me and I told her I would check it out. Told her to stay with Janessa."

"Asher killed his father," I croaked out. "I walked in on the guards trying to kill him, but he overpowered them, and when I was about to go for help, Prince Asher came in and shot him."

Jabo cursed under his breath. "Come on; we need to get you out of here."

"How?" I asked trying to force my eyes to stay focus.

"How do you think I got down here. I grew up here. I know all of the secret passageways. I have another way for us to get out."

He stood and helped me to my feet. I screamed. I had forgotten about my ankle and fell forward.

"What happened? Are you ok?

"My ankle." I bit out leaning on him. "I think I broke it."

"Get on my back then," he said.

"What?" I blinked.

He held my face in his hand, and I tried to focus on his face but I was in so much pain, and I was so tired, I couldn't focus on him.

"I need you to get on my back. I need to carry you out of here. We will get out of here faster if I carry you." He turned and stooped slightly, and I climbed on his back as best as I could and leaned my head down and blinked back a few tears, the last time I had a piggyback ride was years ago…, with my dad.

"How are we getting out of here?" I asked as I struggled to keep it together.

"The same way I came in."

We walked down some stairs that looked as though they were held together by tape. At the bottom of the stairs, there were small puddles of water. "They haven't used these dungeons in close to eighty years. They aren't big on upkeep." He explained.

"Won't they know to look this way?" I asked.

"Probably," Jabo said. "But that won't be for a while, and they won't be able to tell which way we are going." We stopped in front a long brick wall that was closed in. He ran his hand against the wall pressing against different stones. He pressed on the third stone on the fifth row down. The stone gave a small hissing noise and slid back into the wall giving us a small passageway. Jabo didn't waste any time and walked straight through the opening as the door closed behind us.

~

"What's happened since I've been locked up?" I asked as he walked down the hallway, I was trying to stay awake, but I knew I was fighting a losing battle.

I felt Jabo tense.

"Just tell me," I half whispered, half yawned.

He sighed. "The council has been destroyed." It seems as though the coup from Elendil is spreading.

"Nasol? Vikram?" I asked before I could stop myself.

I felt his shoulders droop slightly. "I don't know. I tried reaching out once you went missing and we never received word back. Then we received word of the explosion. No survivors have been reported though no one is allowed within a hundred miles of the wreckage. If anyone did survive, we would have no way of contacting or getting to them."

I squeezed my eyes shut fighting back the tears. "What about the other planets on the council?" I asked.

"No one knows who to trust right now, there have been attacks and coups attempts on ten other planets in the system. With the fighting spread out it's not possible to send help to one planet over another. We need to find out who is behind this, who planned this."

I shook my head. "Your Uncle Asher said he had plans for this system."

"Well, I have a plan now," Jabo said. "We are getting off this planet and away from this mess as fast as we can."

"And go where?" The hallway sloped downwards, and I could hear water splashing in the distance. I looked down, and I saw his feet were immersed in murky brown water. 'This is disgusting.' I thought, thankful my feet were not the ones touching it.

"I don't have that part planned out yet. I just know I need to get my sister, you, and Daneer out of this system as fast as we can."

"Would Earth be an option?" I asked knowing it sounded selfish on my part.

Jabo shrugged. "At this point, anything is possible. But let's worry about getting out of the system safely and then we can worry about where we are going."

"Do you have an idea of where that can be?"

"No, but I need to make sure wherever it will be is safe for us while we monitor this situation."

"I was supposed to be safe here." I murmured. If he heard me, he didn't answer.

He carried me in silence for another few minutes until we came to another stone wall.

"Another secret stone to touch?" I asked, but he shook his head again.

"It's a series of knocks. Otherwise, it could be accidentally opened from the outside by heavy wind or anything like that." He explained. He wrapped his knuckles along a few stones and took a step back. There were a couple of clicks and hissing sounds before the stones folded in on themselves.

Thankfully it was dark outside. I didn't know how we would hide us if the sun was up." I was becoming an expert at escaping life and death situation. Jabo hugged the castle's walls until we reached the edge of the forest and sunk behind some trees.

"Where to now?" I asked.

"To Daneer and Janessa. They were getting the ship ready while I got you. They should be ready by the time we get there," he explained.

"And where is there?"

"About two miles from the castle."

"And you are going to carry me the entire away?"

"Yes," he nodded.

I didn't argue with him. I just laid my head on his back, closed my eyes, and let the sway of his body lull me to sleep.

Chapter Twenty- Seven

When I woke up again, I was in a bed. I shot up and looked around the room. It was small, grey, and cramped. But it was a room and not a cell, so I was happy. It felt like Deja Vu all over again from when I first woke up on the ship with my father standing over me.

But this wasn't like last time – he wasn't here. I felt fresh tears burn my eyes and the weight of my life started to hit me.

I rubbed the tears out of my eyes and felt a small tug on my arm. There was a small IV in my arm that fed from to a small bag filled with a clear liquid. I looked down at my skin and the dirt and grime that covered my body hours ago were gone.

"Abriana?" I didn't hear the door open, but Daneer stood just inside the door.

"Daneer!" I pulled the cover back and scrambled out of bed hissing once my foot touched the floor. She met me halfway, hugged me and helped me back to my bed.

"You were nearly unconsciousness when Jabo finally made it to the ship. We were so worried you weren't going to make it."

"Well, I feel amazing now. Thanks to this." I motioned to the IV in my arm.

"Janessa did that," Daneer beamed. "She's studying or was studying, to be a healer. She should be here soon. We've been checking on you for the last ten hours; you slept for such a long time. I was starting to get worried, but I am glad you are awake."

"Thanks, though I must admit I am tired of waking up like this."

"That time should be over soon." Daneer smiled.

I stretched again and looked around the room again. "Are we out of the system yet?" I asked.

Daneer shook her head. "No, but we are almost there, Jabo said we should cross over in just a few hours."

"I need to speak to them," I said flexing my ankle slightly. It stung a little, but at least I was able to move it. "After I shower, though. I still feel dirty. Where is the bathroom?"

"This way." Daneer smiled as she turned to the door. I held on to the pole my IV was hooked to and limped after her.

We made our way down a small sliver of a hallway a couple of feet until we stopped in front of the narrow door.

"It's much smaller than what you are used to from the castle, but it will do the job just fine."

"Water is water," I said pushing the door open.

"Wait," Daneer said motioning to the IV in my arm. "You need to pull out the IV before you shower."

"Oh, yeah." I held out my arm, and Daneer slowly pulled out the needle. I held my thumb over the hole and pressed down to stop any bleeding. I pulled my thumb back happy to see the puncture wasn't bleeding.

"I'll be here when you get out," Daneer said.

"Thanks," I smiled and walked into the bathroom. She wasn't kidding that it was smaller than what was at the castle, but it was about the same size as the bathroom from my old home.

I slowly undressed and stepped into the shower and turned it on. I stepped fully under the hot water, letting it run over my hair and trickle down to my feet. I leaned up and let the water run over my face. I glanced down at my feet and watched all the dirt still on my body flow down the drain. I reached for the bottle of soap and started washing up.

I wanted to stay under the water for hours, but I didn't know how much water was on the ship and I didn't want to risk using all of it on one shower.

Once I felt clean enough, I turned the water off and stepped out. I grabbed a towel off the rack and started drying off. There were a few black pieces of clothing hanging behind the door, I grabbed them and quickly got a dressed. I turned back to the sink and picked up a packaged toothbrush and brushed my teeth, getting the grime off my teeth. I pushed back my hair and stared at myself in the mirror. I couldn't remember the last time I really looked at myself, studied myself.

I stared into my eyes, my bright, vibrant green eyes. My mother's eyes, my mother skin tone, my mother's hair. Everything about my appearance was all her. I'd always known I looked like her, but now I was living her life – fighting a war, trying to survive. I took a breath and closed my eyes.

She did this. She survived a war. She was able to fight and live through a war. Fight for her people and survive. I never got the chance to really get to know her. It was taken away by Asher, the southern prince, and whoever else they were working with. I opened my eyes and stared at myself once more. I was her daughter, not in just looks alone.

I opened the bathroom door, and Daneer was sitting across from me on the floor.

"Feel better?" She asked, looking me up and down.

"Yes," I nodded.

"Good," she beamed. "Jabo and Janessa are in the front of the ship. We will head there now." She turned, and I followed.

It was a short walk to the front. The ship seemed a bit bigger than the one Nasol, Vikram, and I took to Enia. We walked up a small flight of stairs, down another hall, and we were in the front of the ship. Both Jabo and Janessa were sitting in the front seats. Jabo was steering the ship, and Janessa sat in the other chair looking over some maps on the screen.

"You're awake!" Janessa smiled as she scrambled to stand up before rushing over to hug me. "How are you feeling?" She held me at arm's length as she looked me over. "How's your ankle?"

"Overall I feel good. My ankle feels so much better."
I smiled.

"Glad to see you are doing well," Jabo stood and
swept me up in a hug.

"Thanks to you all," I said once Jabo let me back
down. "I can't thank you enough for finding me. I thought I
was going to die down there."

"I meant to ask; how did you get out? You weren't in
the cell when I found you."

"I realized my cell was made of dirt and that I could
dig myself out. I started to dig once I realized that. When the
floor of the tunnel started to give, I found that I wasn't on the
lowest level. So, I made an opening where the ground was
thinnest, and I jumped down. That's when I hurt my ankle."

"You dug yourself out?" Jabo asked astonished.
"You're resourceful, hold on to that. We will need it where
we are going."

"And where is that?" I asked, hungry for information.

Jabo, Janessa, and Daneer shared a look. "We don't
know."

"What do you mean you don't know?" I asked.

"The main goal is to get outside of the system. From
there, we need to watch and see if a resistance starts to form,"
Jabo said. "Since the destruction of the council, everything is

in utter chaos, and we don't know who we can trust. The wise move is to wait."

"Why don't we start it then, the resistance??" I asked.

"It's not that easy," Jabo said. "From a military standpoint, our war will be over before it began."

"I don't like not doing anything," I said. "I'm tired of doing nothing and waiting."

"Neither do we," Janessa said. "But where can we go? We have no allies in the outer system and no known allies in this system. We have nowhere to set up the foundations of a resistance."

I sighed and leaned back in my chair trying to think of a new plan. "Who are my grandparents?" I asked remembering what the guards said to me.

"What?" Janessa asked. "That's a weird question. Why does it matter now?"

"That's why he kept me alive. Prince Asher said that I had connections I was ignorant of," I explained. "I asked the guards why they were keeping me alive and they said it had to do with my grandparents – my mother's parents. He wanted to keep me alive to use as a bargaining chip. That must mean they are alive and are in a position to be bargained with, right? Otherwise, I should be dead."

"I thought they were dead honestly," Jabo spoke up. "I heard it was quite the scandal."

"What do you mean?" I pressed.

Jabo shrugged and rubbed the back of his neck. "I don't know the whole story just bits and pieces. I was told your grandparents were the leaders of a group that opposed Nasol's family's rule of Elendil. They had spent some time on Earth, and other planets and they wanted the royal family to step down to allow the people to pick their next leader. They had a huge following, but one protest went too far, and they were banished from the planet. The entire family was. It was why your mother was on Earth – she was ousted from the planet – and she lost her rank in the military as well."

"Does that mean they are on Earth?" I asked, slightly hopeful.

Jabo shrugged. "No idea. From what I was told, your mother didn't leave with them. She wanted to go alone."

"So...they could still be alive and willing to support me-us?"

"Again, I have no idea, and more importantly, we have no idea where they may be."

"Is there a photo of them?"

Jabo pressed a few buttons on the screen, and a small photo appeared. I glanced down at the photo. The couple looked young, so the photo had to be old. They were standing in front of a large crowd, and they both were yelling, but there was something familiar about them. Like I'd seen them before.

"Holy crap!" I gasped realizing why they looked so familiar to me. But this couldn't be right; there was no way. "I know them!"

"You do?" Daneer finally spoke up.

"Yeah." I nodded. "They *are* on Earth. They live in my neighborhood. Hell, for my last few birthdays they gave me cake and they always waved to me and….," I trailed off realizing how much they did to have contact with me.

"Are you sure?" Jabo asked.

I nodded. "I'm positive. We can go to Earth! We can go to them!"

"I won't really fit in on Earth," Daneer said motioning to her skin tone. "And I don't want to have to bend light around me twenty-four seven."

"We'll figure it out," I promised. "But right now, I think our best bet is to head to Earth. We could be safe there at least for a bit."

"I don't know," Janessa shook her head. "It seems too easy."

"In what way?" I asked.

"I don't know." she shrugged. "But it just seems too easy I think."

"Look," Jabo spoke up. "I like it. Besides, we have nowhere else to go. This is the best option we have. I think we should go there and see if they are willing to help. Plus, you have your father's side of the family there, right?"

"Yeah." I nodded feeling bad that the thought of seeing my father's side of the family never crossed my mind. Just a few days ago I would have given anything to see them again. Now they didn't even cross my mind until someone else brought them up. So much in my life that changed in a short amount of time.

"Then it's settled. We are headed to Earth, and we just might be able to be the start to this resistance," Jabo said typing a few coordinates into the board. I felt the ship shift course slightly before straightening out.

"How long until we get there?" I asked sitting up in my seat.

"We should be there in just under a week," Jabo said.

"Do we have enough supplies to make it there?" Janessa asked.

"It will be tight, but I think we can make it work," Daneer explained.

"What do we do in the meantime?" Janessa asked looking around the room.

I took a breath, feeling as my mother's daughters more than ever. "We plan our resistance."

Chapter Twenty-Eight

We flew for a few more days before we made it to the outskirts of Earth's Solar System. It wasn't until I actually saw Earth again that I realized how much I missed it.

"Where did you live?" Jabo asked typing a few buttons on the screen.

"Don't we have to worry about satellites?" I asked.

Janessa shook her head. "No, humans don't have technology advanced enough to pick us up on any radar."

I nodded and typed my home's location into the console, and the ship started to fly in. I gripped the seats as the ship shook slightly as it entered Earth's atmosphere.

"Can we just land, like this?" I asked.

"Yes," Jabo said pressing a few buttons on the console, and the ship started to slow its descent. "I've cloaked the outside. No one on the ground will see a thing."

"Are you sure?" I questioned. "I can just imagine someone with a telescope looking up and finding us."

"I used to do it all the time when I would come to visit my aunt," Janessa said.

"That's right! You spent time on Earth with a distant aunt. Why can't we reach out to her as well?" I asked.

Janessa shook her head. "She died a few years ago."

"Oh, I'm sorry," I said.

"You had no way of knowing," Janessa replied. Jabo flew the ship over the forest outside of my community and landed it in a small opening. We experienced a few bumps as we landed, but what could be expected since the woods were not made for a space ships landing.

"What's the plan?" Daneer asked.

"I go to my grandparent's house and ask them to help us fight back."

"Simple I like it," Jabo nodded.

"It's simple because I don't have a better plan."

"Then let's get to it," Janessa said as she stood up.

"Well, we can't just walk out. I mean I can't, not during the daylight at least. Everyone would recognize me."

"Oh!" Daneer spoke up. "I'm going to take care of that. I can bend the light around us. No one will see us. I told you I wasn't as strong as the other light mages, but I can bend light making us virtually invisible."

"I've seen her do it." Jabo nodded. "It could work, but I think it would be best if you cover all of us. It would look a bit suspicious for us to walk out of the woods…, dressed how we are." He motioned to our outfits. "Do you think you can do it?"

Daneer nodded.

"Ok then." I clapped my hands together. "Let's get to it! We don't have time to waste."

We all stood near the door as we got ready to exit. Daneer clasped her hands and then slowly separated them. A few small balls of light grew between her fingers and floated around us connecting and growing around us.

Daneer smiled. "We can go now."

The door to the ship opened, and we all exited the ship. I motioned towards the community.

"This way," I said.

We walked in silence – even though there wasn't anyone around – but we couldn't allow anyone to overhear us.

The walk was taking longer than planned but while I was here, I needed to do something first.

I needed to see something.

Once we broke through the tree line and I saw it, I felt the air leave my body. I felt a hand reach up and I grabbed it as I struggled to take a breath. I stood there, staring at the remains of my house.

"Abriana?" Janessa whispered trying to grab my attention.

"They didn't tear it down." I covered my mouth trying to stifle my sobs looking up at the start of this mess. The top floor of my house was gone, and what was left were charred remains. The living room windows were blown out and the siding was all charred. Half of the front door was burned and missing.

"Is this-" Daneer trailed off as I nodded. I stepped forward again, and the rest followed. I walked around the house to the front gate.

I smiled as I saw the front gate was filled with teddy bears, candles, and signs saying they missed my father and me. "Our car is still here," I said pointing to the old beat up Jeep sitting in front of the house.

"Abriana," Jabo said as he grabbed my hand. "We don't have time for this. We need to go."

I took a breath and nodded. "They live a few streets over." I gave my house one more look before turning away and heading down the street. Everyone followed closely behind me.

We fell into a comfortable silence until I came up to the house.

The Coopers.

They weren't in front of their house working on their yard as usual but, seeing as the day was getting late, they probably retired inside for the rest of the evening.

"I thought it would be bigger?" Janessa remarked looking at the single level home.

"It could be larger on the inside," I said. "I never actually been inside."

I took a deep breath and walked up to the door as everyone followed behind me. I stepped up on the stoop and rapped my knuckles on the door.

We waited a few seconds, and we could hear movement behind the door. There was a bit more shuffling on the other side, and it was a few more moments before the door opened.

Mr. Cooper stood facing us and very shortly Mrs. Cooper joined him. For the first time since I met her, I truly looked at her.

I had her high cheekbones and his bright green eyes and nose. I felt my eyes water as my grandmother smiled at me.

"Abriana." She gasped. "You're alive."

"Hi." I waved as fresh tears filled my eyes. "Can we come in?"

Mrs. Copper nodded, reached out a hand, and I took it.

Chapter Twenty-Nine

We were gathered inside their living room the Coopers, or my grandparents I wasn't sure what to call them yet.

If I had ever come in before I would have known what my mother looked like years ago. The wall was filled with photos of her throughout her life.

I looked so much like her. I stared at another one of her photos when she looked to be my age. We could have passed for sisters.

For a brief moment, I let myself think of what could have been if she never left, or better yet if she was still here. If this had never happened and she just came back, and we were never attacked.

I wondered if this war was never started and we never left Earth. Would my life be so different? Would I have accepted her as I did on the ship?

Would she have talked to her parents and would she have introduced us?

I shook my head clearing my mind of those thoughts. There was no use to dwelling on thoughts and actions that could never happen.

"You have no idea how wonderful it is to see you. To actually be able to talk to you." Mrs. Cooper my grandmother said walking back into the room with a few papers in her hands. Her husband was not far behind her carrying a large tray of drinks and small sandwiches. "For so long we've had to watch you grow up on the sidelines of your life. You look so much like her."

"Thank you, Mrs. Cooper." I smiled.

"Don't" She shook her head reaching up and cupped my cheek with her free hand. "Don't call me Mrs. Cooper. Call me Alana darling."

"And call me Akriam." Mr. Cooper smiled.

"Yes, thank you. I will." I smiled wiping a stray tear. "Oh, and these are my friends!" I said turning to face them. "This is Janessa, Jabo, and Daneer." I motioned, and they wave or nodded when I mentioned their name.

"It's wonderful to meet you all," Alana said. "Please feel free to take a seat.

Akriam placed the tray down on the coffee table sat down on the love seat, and Alana sat down next to him and placed her papers down on the table. Janessa and Jabo sat on the longer couch to their left. Daneer sat in one of their wingback chairs across from them, and I sat down in the other.

"Do you know what is happening?" Jabo asked cutting straight to the point. Janessa reached forward and grabbed a bottle water off the tray and drank it down.

Akriam nodded. "We still have contacts all throughout the system, so we have been able to keep a close eye on the situation." He took a deep breath. "We know that the system is falling into chaos."

"What do you plan to do about it?" I asked.

They shared a quick look between them, but Alana answered. "We haven't planned to do anything yet."

"What, why not you have!" I shot up. "They killed my parents, your daughter! You must want to fight back. You can't let this happen..."

Alana held up a hand stopping my tirade short. "I didn't say we weren't planning at all, I said yet."

"Oh." I felt heat rush to my cheeks, and I sat back down, once again I spoke without thinking.

"We are waiting to receive word from more of our contacts. We will need to know who we can trust as our allies in the coming war." Alana said.

"With the system in turmoil, we cannot trust one planet over another," Akriam said.

"What do you suppose we do?" Jabo asked.

"We have contacts who are outside of the Isildur system," Alana said. "From the free worlds."

"You can't be serious." Janessa cut in. "You want to involve another system in this war? That's crazy. If they jump in, they will want to absorb the Isildur System into their own."

"I understand," Alana nodded. "but without help how do you suggest you will gain the numbers and money needed to take back control? Our best option and the best plan is to reach out to people with the resources we need. If we work with the free worlds, they won't care to rule. They will want to help the planets rule freely. One where the people will choose their rulers and have a say in who governors them."

"Most of the planets in the Isildur System won't go for that," Janessa said.

"They won't have a choice," Alana said. "They either accept our help, or they die by the hands of those trying to oppress them. I think they will take the help if they have the chance to be free."

"When do you think they will be able to help?" I asked.

"They are still deciding if they want to give aid and support the fight and if so how much they are willing to give. We will need them to back us financially during this time. Wars are expensive and impossible to win without outside support. But our contacts are confident that they will decide in our favor."

"I understand that, but I'm not sure if bringing another system into our mess is the best option," Janessa said.

"It's the only option you have," Alana said. "And I think you would rather have a say with them during the planning stages than to be on the outside looking in."

Janessa looked as though she wanted to retort but kept her mouth shut. I was currently in awe of these people; my grandparents were about to start the resistance. I could see where my mother got it, and where I did.

"But either way we are glad you are here." Alana continued. "We were leaving shortly to go meet our contacts."

"You were?" I asked.

"Yes, we were waiting for a few of members to make the final arrangements over the next few days. We are scheduled to leave in three days."

"How many members do you have living on earth?" I asked.

Alana paused to think about it. "We have about twenty members of our resistance here."

"And what preparations still need to be made?" Daneer asked.

"We have kept our ships up to date for years, but we will need fuel and food for the journey. It takes time to get enough in storage for a long journey." Akriam explained. "We will now need to make sure we will have enough fuel and food for your four as well."

"I do have a question," I said.

"Anything dear," Alana said.

"Have you heard anything about my father's family, about how they are doing?" I asked. "What's is being said about the attack?"

"Oh dear," Alana said. "It's not good." She pulled out her phone and typed a few buttons on the screen and handed it over to me. "Take a look."

I peered down at the screen at the news article, the tagline 'Gas Main explosions kills Father and Daughter.'

"They are saying it was a gas main?"

"It was the only explanation they could come up with that could explain the level of damage to the house," Akriam said. "And why they didn't find any bodies."

"What about my family, my father's family?" I asked again.

"They had a wonderful service for you both," Akriam said. "Alana and I went, and we have seen them since, they are hurting, but they are getting through this."

I nodded feeling a small weight I hadn't realize I was carrying lift; it was good to hear they were getting through this.

"So, three days," I said changing the subject back to the task at hand. "That's when we leave?"

"Yes, our members will be here tomorrow to start making final preparations to leave. They will be happy to meet you Abriana, and your friends and that you all have survived and made it here. There were not many people who were able to escape the carnage. It will be good to have somewhat of an inside view into the making of this chaos."

"Well we do not know everything, but I think we do know enough to help," Jabo said.

"Every little bit helps," Akriam said.

I sighed and leaned back in my chair and closed my eyes. Flashes of my father, mother, Vikram, and Nasol's faces played in repeat under my eyelids. I was going to help avenge their deaths and the death of everyone who has died in this coup.

I was going to make Asher, Borran and everyone else involved in this coup pay. I was going to kill them all.

More by The Author

Sasha lived a simple life until her mother's secret came to light. Now, at the age of sixteen, Sasha learns that, not only has everything to that point been a lie, but now there's a hit squad after her. To escape their attackers, Sasha's mother, Jasmine, sacrifices herself so her daughter can escape. With her best friend Cassie in tow, and her mother branded a traitor to the crown Sasha must seek out the aunt she never knew for the protection she now needs. She hopes with the help of her aunt, she can unravel her mother's history and prove her innocence. Though the more she digs the more she wishes for this to be a terrible dream. As she uncovers her mother's greatest lie she is faced with a decision that will not only change her life but also the entire kingdom.

Adalithiel is a modern magical coming of age story for you not so typical teenager.

About the Author

 **ANDREA ROSE WASHINGTON** loves all stories that include fantasy, paranormal, science fiction or mystery. She prefers to read and write stories with a non-traditional viewpoint and strong female lead. She's never without a book in her hand and she works tirelessly to bring characters that look like her to print.

For more information about Andrea check out her website.

Website: www.ARWBooks.com

Made in USA - Kendallville, IN
66548_9781720030676
08.10.2023 1308